AN IMPRO... NT

Pommy felt Justi... caressingly from c... ...ht, hear the blood pou... ...toward her. She felt the kiss in his eyes as though his lips had already taken possession of hers. She understood the hunger she saw in his eyes, for that same need swept her in wordless demand.

Pommy, of course, was engaged to another man, the odious Frederick Watters. And Justin was engaged to another woman, the insipid Anilee Mortimer.

What they were engaged in now, though, was something else. Something very close to scandal . . .

VANESSA GRAY grew up in Oak Park, Illinois, and graduated from the University of Chicago. She currently lives in the farm country of northeastern Indiana, where she pursues her interests in the history of Georgian England and the Middle Ages. She is the author of a number of bestselling Regencies available in Signet editions.

Best-Laid Plans

Vanessa Gray

A SIGNET BOOK

SIGNET
Published by the Penguin Group
Penguin Books USA Inc., 375 Hudson Street,
New York, New York 10014, U.S.A.
Penguin Books Ltd, 27 Wrights Lane,
London W8 5TZ, England
Penguin Books Australia Ltd, Ringwood,
Victoria, Australia
Penguin Books Canada Ltd, 2801 John Street,
Markham, Ontario, Canada L3R 1B4
Penguin Books (N.Z.) Ltd, 182-190 Wairau Road,
Auckland 10, New Zealand

Penguin Books Ltd, Registered Offices:
Harmondsworth, Middlesex, England

First published by Signet, an imprint of New American Library, a
division of Penguin Books USA Inc.

First Printing, November, 1990
10 9 8 7 6 5 4 3 2 1

BOOKS ARE AVAILABLE AT QUANTITY DISCOUNTS WHEN USED TO
PROMOTE PRODUCTS OR SERVICES. FOR INFORMATION PLEASE WRITE
TO PREMIUM MARKETING DIVISION, PENGUIN BOOKS USA INC.,
375 HUDSON STREET, NEW YORK, NEW YORK 10014.

1

The rumble of thunder far to the west of London gave pause to Miss Melpomene Fiske, who was at the moment stealing silently from the house of her father's cousin Lydia, Lady Derwent, in Berkeley Square.

Perhaps it would be safer, in light of the unpromising weather, to postpone her impromptu travel plans until the next night. She held her hooded cloak tight at her throat with one hand and all her possessions that she thought she could carry wrapped in a shawl in the other. She stood in the center of her bedroom while she considered. But the recollection of Frederick's last remark, not meant for her ears, brought burning mortification to her cheeks and a certain desperation to her mind.

"Believe me," young Mr. Watters—he of the wet kiss and damp hands—had told his mother, with force, "the only thing worse than marrying the girl would be to be thrown in debtors' prison."

No, her need to escape was too urgent to be frightened off by the prospect of receiving a drenching, or even by the possibility of dying from congestion on the chest due to sitting in sodden garments for hours on the public stagecoach.

Pommy blew out the single candle and looked through the

uncurtained window. Berkeley Square, lit only by the newly installed gaslights, was empty, save for the shadows cast by the shrubs around the iron fence. No person walked along the pavement, no carriage wheels rumbled, no shod horses' hooves disturbed the silence.

Only thunder, now a little closer, and far away the cry of the watchman, disturbed the dark peace.

Pommy, however, was far from tranquil in her mind. Her resolve almost failed—almost. Reminding herself firmly that this very day—since it was already past midnight—her name would appear in the *Gazette* as betrothed to her cousin Frederick Watters, she picked up her bundle by the tied ends and stepped out into the hall.

She listened for a moment. Only the ordinary sounds of a sleeping household came to her ears. Delicately, remembering the two particular steps prone to squeak under pressure, she descended like a shadow to the ground floor. She had not before seen these rooms lit only by the gaslights on the square, and they seemed alien to her. Illumination filtered faintly through the dawn curtains. Chairs cast unexpected and elongated shadows and doors opened onto mysteriously vague vistas. She was forced to be quite firm with her quaking knees.

Fortunately, her escape route was already fixed in her mind. She crossed the hall to the library. The dying fire, reacting to the sudden draft from the open door, flared dimly and an ember dropped softly into the ashes. A sound fit to wake the dead, she thought, or at least her sleeping cousins. No sound came from upstairs.

She had only a few more steps to take. She must go through the French doors onto the terrace at the side of the house, cross to the marble balustrade and climb it, and descend to the ground by means of a heavily vined trellis. Then she must make her way to the Swan with Two Necks on Gresham

Street and take the morning stage to Hammondsworth in Middlesex. Anyone there should be able to direct her to Edgecumbe Manor, the residence of her grandmother the dowager Duchess of Woodburn.

Beyond the journey, she dared not think. How the duchess would receive a granddaughter she did not know arriving unannounced on her doorstep did not bear thinking on.

First things first. She took a deep breath and stepped onto the terrace. The sudden chill of the night air, after the warmth of the library, made her shiver.

She cast a countrywoman's weather-wise eye at the sky, but the reflected light of the vast city obscured the stars and veiled the approaching storm clouds. A sharper note of thunder reminded her of the need for haste.

She kept her valuable parcel clutched in one hand while she climbed the low balustrade. For a girl who had climbed every tree on her father's estate in Bedfordshire, the few feet of marble posed no obstacle.

The ancient vine, growing on a wooden trellis, was quite another matter. The trellis crosspiece upon which she set her weight at the first cracked ominously and the vein itself writhed under her foot like a living thing. Immediately she returned to solid marble footing. She stared into the darkness below the terrace, and judged it too far to jump. It would serve no purpose for her to be found in the morning crumpled up with a broken limb! It might take *weeks* for the bone to heal.

Perched atop the balustrade, she eyed her belongings balefully. She thought she packed only necessities, but the bundle loomed in the dark as a great storage trunk. She needed both hands for the descent. There was only one thing to do. She loosened the knot in the shawl and tied the longer ends around her neck. She considered the unsightly bulge on her chest to be in her way, and carefully pulled it around so that it nestled between her shoulder blades.

There was no other way to the ground. She must risk the trellis. She put both hands on the shaky structure, and stepped carefully onto it, carrying some of her weight with her arms. An ominous crack warned her, and she hastily stepped down to a lower crosspiece.

The lattice, groaning softly, held.

Thank goodness, she thought jubilantly. I'm safely away. Nothing can stop me now.

Some moments earlier and only a short distance away, Justin Harcourt, Lord Rutledge, made his deliberate way down Berkeley Street—deliberate, because he was more than ordinarily foxed and, besides, there was nothing at home to entice him to hurry.

He was a man possessed of enormous wealth and superlative social address when he chose to use it, which was seldom, and he had not the slightest pleasure in contemplating his future. His present inebriated condition was one in which he found himself more and more frequently as he saw the jaws of parson's mousetrap opening wide before him.

Betrothed just out of school to a young lady he now took great pains to know only slightly, he found that nothing in his life was worth the doing. This evening, for example, he had spent at Brooks's in gaming, and had won hugely. However, he had scooped his winnings carelessly from the table, bestowed them all on an old woman shambling by on the pavement outside, and sent his carriage home.

"The walk will do me good," he told a friend, "if only the pavement would hold still."

Emerging from St. James's Street onto Piccadilly, he considered his direction. From here, the distance to his rooms in Bruton Street was shorter if he turned to his right and went home by way of Old Bond Street.

In tune with his generally perverse mood, he turned left. In due course he rounded the corner of Berkeley Street and Piccadilly, heading north with commendably steady steps.

Thus it was that as Lord Rutledge approached Berkeley Square, having walked some distance the better to dissipate the effects of wine taken in injudicious amounts, he found the chilly air had, while sobering him somewhat, intensified his dark mood.

He was, and had been, wishful to postpone his wedding as long as possible. The marriage had been arranged while he was enjoying what his tutor, an experienced bear-leader, called "the fleshpots of Europe." Justin's assent had been desired, or rather commanded, of him, and without serious thought it was given.

Now Anilee's father, the redoubtable Sir Henry Mortimer, had recently taken to dropping massive hints, and Justin knew that his doom was inevitable. In fact, a large house party was planned for a fortnight hence, at Lord Rutledge's own family seat, Lisle Court in Middlesex, at which his family and Anilee's would be present, and the formal and public announcement of the betrothal and approaching wedding would take place.

Even more than a sufficiency of distinguished port had not lifted Justin's spirits. It was at this moment that the melody of a lugubrious Russian folk song entered his mind. The song had been a favorite of the exceedingly eccentric Grand Duchess Catherine of Oldenburg, and since the grand duchess detested all other kinds of music, most of London had become familiar with the tune. Lord Rutledge remembered also a few of the words, and never a man to suppress his inclinations, as he came abreast of the iron railing surrounding Lady Derwent's rented house, he began to sing, with no preliminary clearing of the throat, no testing of the pitch.

His clear baritone voice, pleasant of timbre and resonant in carrying quality, struck the unsuspecting Pommy much as a fire bell in the night. In a panic, her foot, reaching for the next foothold, missed. She crashed noisily to the ground, followed by a part of the overburdened trellis, which landed in sections, along with a good part of the vine itself, on top of her.

When she hit the ground, the wind was knocked out of her. For a moment, she could only cower, gasping for breath, in a heap against the foundations of the terrace. Her parcel! It had been jarred loose from around her throat when she fell. Her mother's pearls! In a panic she groped for the necklace, and found it. Mercifully, the knot had not come completely undone, and she tied it more securely.

Who was the singer? And where was he?

She listened intently. The singing had stopped abruptly, and instead of the sounds of footsteps receding into the distance, there was nothing.

She could hear only the mutterings of the approaching storm above the constant sound of the city—a sound unpleasantly reminding her of a beast awakening—and not very far away, a watchman's cry.

Recovering, she began to wonder what had happened to the singer. Had he been as frightened by the sound of her fall as she was? And surely Cousin Lydia and Frederick might be expected to burst from the house, armed against housebreakers.

She had to get away. She wished she were dead rather than have to endure Cousin Lydia's endless sermons on her manifold faults, only a shade less tormenting than Frederick's awkward groping in shadowy corners. But no lights sprang up in the house as yet, and she began to entertain a hope that all would be well, after all.

That hope died. Now she could hear footsteps—approaching softly, stealing toward her. Belatedly she realized her upturned face would shine whitely in the dark, and wished fervently that she had taken time to blacken her face. She and Ned, the vicar's son, had done just so once at Beechknoll when they lay in wait to catch a chicken thief. The miscreant had been after Little Henny, who laid the *best* eggs. They had caught the thief, too.

Just as well she had not thought of disguising herself thus. She probably could not get a seat on the stage in the morning with a face blackened like a highwayman.

The footsteps nearly at hand seemed astonishingly light to belong to the large figure now looming out of the night. He was silhouetted against the lights burning in the square so she could not see anything of him save his size, which was great. Clearly the singer was investigating the crash. He stopped just beside her. She made herself as small as she could, trying to melt into the ground. If her luck held, he would not see her in the shadows.

Her luck might have been in, had not her curiosity come to life and taken over. The man stood motionless for such a long time that her nerves stretched to the breaking point. What was he doing? She moved her head slightly, the better to watch him. Perhaps, finding nothing, he would go away.

Lord Rutledge was faced with a puzzle. He had heard a crash somewhere in this garden, a crash that had followed, unaccountably, upon the heels of his musical effort. But what had caused the crash? The marble terrace, of course, was still intact, and no other immediate cause came to his still-fogged mind.

However, he was convinced that something was truly amiss

here. Crashes of the dimensions of the one he had heard were not commonplace in London, at least not in Berkeley Square. A cat on the prowl? No. Clearly an intruder in this garden—one who had no business here, as he did not himself.

The thought came to him that a proper law-abiding gentleman should rouse the household to danger. But what could he tell them? Besides, he had no idea whose house this was. A house in this square, marble terrace, with what seemed to be some kind of vine growing up directly before him as he stood looking up—the house belonged to no one he knew. He was reluctant to march up to the door, knowing that alcoholic fumes still circled around his head, and warn the unknown householder there was someone in his garden.

Without purpose, his hands moved on the shortened trellis. His fingers came abruptly upon the sharp splinters left from Pommy's accident, and a clear and pungent oath marked the occasion.

The intruder had approached near enough so Pommy could have reached out and touched his cloak. What was he doing here? Why didn't he leave?

Curious, Pommy forgot her position and moved abruptly. The movement and, quite likely, her upturned face a white smudge around his knees caught his eye.

All came clear to Lord Rutledge in that moment. Some thieving footman had fallen into his hands, probably a manservant eloping with the family's silver, who by great ill fortune had fallen into the virtuous clutches of Lord Rutledge, member of the House of Lords and a sworn upholder of law and order.

Exultantly he stooped to grasp whatever part of the villain came to hand. He found a fold of woolen serge and an arm within, and he pulled the culprit up. Grasping the slight figure before him by both arms, he stood his quarry upright before him and cursed the dim light that revealed so little of the thief.

Lord Rutledge was a cultivated man with well-spoken ways, not usually at a loss for words, but at this moment, holding a thief caught red-handed, his accustomed address failed him. It seemed to him, as the silence grew, that someone ought to say something.

Manfully, through fumes of well-aged port lingering in his brain, he utterd the only words that seemed to suit the occasion. On a note of triumph, he exclaimed, ''Aha!''

His victim suddenly became deadweight, and he nearly lost his grip. ''Don't try that,'' he said sharply. The culprit was small, reaching only to the middle of his chest. The faint scent of lavender puzzled him. Surely a footman would not be so nice of habit?

He shook his victim. ''What have you in your hands? Here, give it to me.''

Pommy clutched her shawl-wrapped parcel. She dared not give it up. It contained what she considered necessary for running away from home and, like a talisman against ill fortune, included her pearls, of great value both sentimental and real. Before her captor could open his mouth again, she hissed, ''Quiet! You'll rouse the house.''

Too late she realized that must be exactly his intent. She writhed in his grip. Escape was her only hope now.

Caught unaware by her quick movement, Justin almost lost her. Gathering her arms and pulling her to him in a gigantic but unaffectionate hug, he said, unconsciously lowering his voice, ''So you're trying to get away. I was right: the footman running off with the spoons. Lucky for your mistress that I caught you.''

Pommy, however, was not resigned to being caught. Too much was at stake here. Her entire life at the least, she believed, and no arrogant passerby, even though by his voice she believed him to be a gentleman, was going to interfere in her desperate escape.

She had had enough of gentlemen, thank you! Frederick, for one, with his fumbling advances to make her agree to marry him without "making a fuss," as he described her vigorous protests. And for another, her father, barely conscious at the best of times that he had a daughter, and completely uninterested in her fate, to say nothing of her feelings. If she had been a marble caryatid holding up a Grecian roof, she might have gained his attention.

All these thoughts hurried through her mind like swiftly coursing hares while she was fighting her captor's iron grip on her arms and protecting her small packet of valuables. He was much stronger than she thought. In truth, he was holding her now at arm's length, immobilized, and the wretch wasn't even breathing hard.

One last effort, one lucky blow of her booted foot on his kneecap, and he flinched at the sudden pain. At the same time, involuntarily, his grasp loosened on her, and in a flash she wriggled loose and was gone, running lightly across the lawn.

While she was more familiar with the small grassy plot than her pursuer, and had a good head start on him, he had the advantage of anger to spur him on, as well as a good amount of pain. He put on a fine burst of speed, ignoring his knee, and caught up to her at the gate in the iron fence through which he himself had entered only a few minutes since, to fall into the bizarre situation in which he now found himself.

Catching up to his quarry at the gate, Justin took hold of a shoulder, swung his captive around, and thrust the escaping footman against the wall of the stables. Gone was his gentle manner. He resolved to subdue the thief once and for all. He shoved him hard against the wall and reached to remove the concealing cloak.

"Uncover your head, villain. So I can see your ugly face.

I'll take care to know you again, you may be sure. What? You won't? Stop sniveling, coward. You'll be well taken care of in Newgate, I warrant you. Off with this garment . . .''

So saying, he pressed his thighs against the legs of his victim and reached roughly to find and loosen the strings of Pommy's cloak.

''Stop struggling. I would be reluctant to plant you a leveler just to keep you quiet for the watch . . .''

It was then that, with his body pinning his victim against the wall and his hands busy, he made the most astonishing discovery of this bizarre night.

''Good God! You're female.''

2

Pommy's spirits plummeted. She shrank from his exploring hands on her, roughly intrusive as she supposed was reasonable when dealing with criminals. Now her last disguise was penetrated and the fat was in the fire, unless . . .

"Aha," he cried again, this time in mistaken triumph. "Not the footman, but the upstairs maid. Now let me see what jewels you have in that precious parcel of yours."

He had no right, she thought. She was desperate to get away. The night was more than half gone, and she had a long way to go to reach the stagecoach yard. She clung to her parcel. She had almost got away before, and she could do it again. This time he knew she was female, and that circumstance might be used in her favor.

He did not intend to let her elude him. He held her easily with one hand, while with the other he searched for the parcel he knew she had hidden somewhere about her person. She had thrust it behind her between her back and the wall. The sharp corner of her modest jewel case protruded uncomfortably into the small of her back. She was abruptly aware of his scent, a not-unpleasant mixture of soap and liquor, and unaccountably she stopped struggling for a moment, listening to a small riot of bewildering emotions developing within her.

With an effort she stifled the rebellion. It now seemed more urgent than ever to get away from him. Thunder muttered much closer now, and the watchman's cry sounded in the next street.

She had the first time almost made it out the gate. It was not so easy this time. His hard body was still pressed against hers, in an intimacy she dared not think of. An indignity, to be sure, and at another time she might wish to point out her displeasure at his unwonted liberties, but just at the moment she had too much on her mind.

Her imagination, generally lively, now ran riot. If he gave her up to the watch, as he gave every intimation he would do, she was undone. She would be brought up before the Beak. Where did she hear such a vulgar expression? The Beak would send her to Newgate, and she would be thrown in among criminals, and Cousin Lydia would wash her hands of her—and rightly so.

Or, if she escaped being sent to prison, this terrible man could easily drag her to the front door of the house, rouse the household, and Cousin Lydia would wash her hands of her.

Either way, she would be ruined.

With an uncommon burst of strength, she took him by surprise. Kicking out again at him, she slid out of his reach and sped toward the gate once more. His clutch, however, did not reach her, but his fingers closed on the shawl, and as she ran, she heard it tear. Clinging to it desperately to save the contents, she lost her advantage, and before she reached the gate, she was recaptured.

But this time the gentleman as sorely tried. He had not given a fig for the valuables clearly being removed from the house in whose yard he stood now. He had come upon the thief not by design but more or less by chance, and now he was heartily weary of the whole imbroglio. If this were what excessive indulgence in spirits brought one to, he might with justification consider becoming a total abstainer.

"I do not blame you for escaping," he told her, "but I might be tempted to let you go." Hope leapt in Pommy's heart, but only for a moment, for he added, "I must be sure there are no valuables in this parcel you cling to so tightly. You can see my dilemma? Since you won't give me your name and you've not said a word, you must realize that I have my duty to perform."

She said nothing. She was aware that only a few words from her would reveal she was certainly no servant, and while she believed she could avoid being sent to Newgate, yet the alternative, of being delivered in disgrace to Frederick Watters, was hardly more appealing.

But he must not find the jewel case. The pearls were her own and she had every right to remove them from the house, but to prove that would probably mean bringing Cousin Lydia and quite likely Frederick as well into the matter.

Unconsciously, she moaned.

"But, child," he said in the voice of reason, "where would we all be if everyone took everyone else's property?"

As a coherent argument, his words lacked something, he considered. Any of his friends would have been amazed to hear such a rackety question coming from such a gallant.

Where would they be, indeed? thought Pommy. If she were unmasked, she had little hope that Cousin Lydia would forgive her, even less hope that she could escape marriage with that odious Frederick. And she knew beyond doubt that she would be allowed no further chance to escape.

Maybe, if she explained to this man, he would be merciful. She could but try. She opened her lips to tell him: her name, her reasons for climbing, or rather falling, down the trellis in the dark of night. But she was exhausted, frightened, and overset, and her lips quivered. She dared not speak for a moment, lest she lose her shaky self-control, such as it was, and start to cry. To weep was a sign of a weakness so lowering she did not wish even to think about it.

Lord Rutledge was completely unaware of the turmoil rushing through Pommy's thoughts. He had been well cast-away when he left the club, and the cool air had begun the work of restoration. But then came this strange incident through which he found himself clutching a maidservant in some unknown's garden. And why did time pass so slowly? Surely, he had spent the better part of a week inside this fence.

"You haven't said a word. Are you a mute?" he wondered, looking for an excuse to wash his hands of this burden. "Or perhaps a deaf-mute, so that you haven't heard a word I've said?"

He was sobering fast, but there was still a distance to go before he could think coherently, make responsible decisions, even to hope to get rid of his pounding headache. He did know the right thing to do was to restore the maid to her employer, preferably by way of the watch to avoid embarrassing personal explanations, and go on to his rooms in Bruton Street.

But then, his wayward curiosity intervened, pointing out that in that event he would never know the outcome. Who was this person, what was she stealing, and whose house was now lacking some of its valuables?

Suddenly decision was snatched from his grasp. He had left it too long.

From almost under his feet, so it seemed, came the gin-hoarse voice of the watchman, crying, "Two hours past midnight."

Pommy, startled, acted quickly. She had forgotten the watch was so near. Convulsively, she clutched at her captor's cloak in a muddled attempt to hide herself. Remembering how her upturned face in the darkness had brought her this gentleman's unwanted attention, she buried her face in his chest and pressed herself close enough to him to hear his quickened breathing.

She heard, too, the heavy footsteps of the watchman coming close, closer . . . and stop.

With commendable promptitude, Lord Rutledge responded. Perhaps his mind was already made up. Duty required that he turn her over to the watch, and the watchman was at hand. A word from him and his dilemma would be solved. The wench deserved nothing from him, no consideration, no mercy.

He rose to the demands of necessity. With one hand at the back of Pommy's head, feeling with a shock of pleasure the crisp curls beneath his fingers, with his other hand he swept the long folds of his evening cloak around her, completely enveloping her.

Her ringlets were yielding and clean to his touch, and the slender person hidden from the world by the soft wool broadcloth of his cloak trembled closely against him like a frightened bird. Sensations not unfamiliar to Lord Rutledge flooded him, but this time they seemed mingled with a kind of protective tenderness that surprised him.

This was no time, he decided, for analysis, to discover why this thieving and silent upstairs maid should arouse such gentle emotions in him.

The watch was upon them. Rutledge had been as aware as Pommy that the watchman had stopped on the pavement a few feet away. Rutledge could hear the heavy breathing close at hand, against the background of a sharp roll of thunder.

The watchman lifted his lantern to shoulder height. Illumination fell only on Rutledge's cheek and shoulder. The watch peered at him. Knowing how little privacy was to be found in the servants' quarters of the great houses on the square, he believed he had discovered merely a clandestine tryst of the kind common to the lower orders. However, he had his job to do.

"Here, here, what's all this?" he cried. "Fine goings-on right here in the street."

The watchman was not new to his rounds. He was proof against much that was shocking. He took in his stride dead or drunken bodies in the street, stray dogs fighting to the death, and certainly he was not flustered by a pair of amorous servants seeking pleasure in a darkened garden.

But suppose, he argued to himself, a nightpad were stealing away with valuables from one of those great houses he was paid to guard, and the thief not be caught by the watch? It would be the end of his employment for a certainty, and he dared not chance it.

"Here, here," he repeated on a more demanding note.

Lord Rutledge's wits were fast returning to him. There was only one effective way to deal with the night watchman, and he did so at once.

"Damn your eyes! How dare you interfere with a gentleman's pleasure. Get on about your business."

This spirited response was followed in the same arrogant but hushed voice by a turn of vulgar phrase that struck admiration in the heart of the watchman. A proper gentleman, after all, he realized, and welcomed a few words he hadn't heard before but would commit to memory before the night was over.

"Good night, my lord," he said with respect, and moved hastily on.

Now that the present danger was past, Lord Rutledge, being a man of honor, could be expected to release his prisoner. Instead, he captured the fluttering hand, seemingly caught inside his waistcoat.

Pommy, whose last few moments had been trying indeed, breathed a sigh of relief. How thankful she was to her adversary that he had helped her and not betrayed her.

She lifted her glance to him. But before she could speak her gratitude, his lips found hers. They were warm and insistent, tasting oddly of wine and tobacco.

Sheer amazement at this unexpected turn of events held her quiet at first. Then, as his lips moved to her cheek, the exquisite sensation of being nibbled by butterflies held her captive even more than his encircling arms, at least for a while. She did not try to pull away for a long moment. Indeed, one arm moved—entirely on its own, of course—until it lay around his neck.

The full horror of her situation burst on her. She knew well what any well-brought-up young lady could allow, and in no manner could these past few minutes be included. Shamed she was, of course, in large part because she had enjoyed those few minutes. Disgracefully, she was reluctant to pull away. Cousin Lydia would swoon away, could she see her young charge now.

But she had not fled Cousin Lydia's house without reason, and while she had momentarily lost sight of her goal, it came back clear and clamoring for attention. The stagecoach would soon be preparing to set out on a long day's run, and she must be on it, no matter how.

Pommy, gathering her wits as best she might, was guided by desperation. No longer was she trying to disguise her quality. In fact, she had already forgotten that her voice, if she spoke above the whisper she had employed thus far, would betray her. To tell truth, the logic by which she had acted this evening had unaccountably deserted her. She did not see anything strange, even in these circumstances, in displaying a wild adherence to civility.

"Thank you, sir, for not betraying me to the watch. I am

extremely grateful to you. Now, if you please, allow me to—''

Lord Rutledge still held her body close to his, stroking her soft hair with his free hand. However, upon hearing the unmistakable accents of a gently bred female, he jerked his hands away from her as if they had been scalded, and sprang back. His glare, had she been able to see it in the darkness, was hot enough to melt the buttons on her walking dress, but at least she was free.

"You are not a serving wench," he accused her after a fruity oath.

"Hush. You'll draw the watch back."

He gave no sign of hearing her, but he lowered his voice. "You deceived me."

At least she had shocked him! Stagecoach forgotten, she felt required to give this too-forward gentleman a set-down. She applied herself to the task. "I never did," she whispered fiercely. "You assumed, just as you assumed I had the family silver in my shawl. It never occurred to you, I suppose, that a silver coffee set would weigh pounds and would be too big to carry off in such a small package?"

She did not understand herself. Fearful of being stopped by the watch, uncertain in the extreme about her future, beset by unhappiness and doubts, she had held the conviction that she stood alone against the world.

Now in the last few moments, something had subtly changed. Optimism made its unwarranted appearance. After all, she had not been turned over to the watch. It was within reason to believe it possible that she might get to the inn yard before the stage left at daybreak. It was even possible, she thought, that this long, miserable night might eventually come to an end. Any or all of these considerations might have been credited with the lightening of her spirits.

Never, never would she have admitted that the presence

of her self-appointed protector from the watch, no matter how temporary his company, might have anything to do with the sudden rosy shimmer that surrounded her.

Indeed, she felt impelled to point out, in case her first remark had gone unnoticed, his lack of logic. "I have to inform you that Lyd—that the silver from that house is far more massive than I could carry off in a cart."

Heedless of her argument, he demanded, "Who are you? And who is the lady you almost mentioned? Let's take you home and find out just who, and what, you are."

He had not even yet taken her measure. Unless he held her in a viselike grip, she as not his to order about.

"Not to that house," she hissed hotly, writhed eellike away, and ran.

She had reached the iron gate before she looked back over her shoulder to see where her pursuer was, how close on her heels.

Surprisingly he was back at the stable wall, making not the slightest move to come after her.

At last she was truly free! Conscious of a small regret that he could so suddenly change his mind and lose all interest in her, she told herself that the only remaining barrier left before her was the long walk to the coaching inn.

While she paused at the gate, looking back at her recent captor, he slowly lifted one hand as though in salute. And in that one hand, he held aloft the shawl-wrapped parcel containing a few garments, her tiny fund of coins, her mother's pearls, and a small wrapped cake to tide her over until she reached her unsuspecting grandmother in Middlesex.

Slowly she retraced her steps and held out her hand for her belongings. Rutledge lounged against the stable wall. He was so tall that he could easily keep the small parcel out of her reach over his head. For a moment, he was put forcibly in mind of the juvenile game of keep-away. He did not remember enjoying the game so much.

He was by now exceedingly curious as to this small young lady with whom he had become enmeshed. He could not turn her over to the watch: she was clearly too well-bred. He thought ruefully that he had not known her quality until the last few moments, but he had not betrayed her even so.

It would have been the proper action of a prudent man to have washed his hands of her, but Justin Harcourt, Lord Rutledge, was a man who saw his future in darker shades of gray. He would have to see this through. It occurred to him that she must be in a good deal of trouble. Clearly she was making her escape from a situation intolerable to her. She did not seem to be without intelligence. When she had ripped up at him, she had certainly spoken to the point.

An odd notion came to him, stirring at the back of his mind. There was a word for this young lady. Damn his hazy brain! He'd think of it in a moment—something to do with dragons. Damsel in distress, that was it. And he was clearly her knight-errant and must save her from who knew what. That settled to his satisfaction, he felt easier with her.

It was not wonderful that he did not recognize her even though she as a lady of quality. His taste did not take him to the brilliant lights, the glittering salons of London. Besides disliking fashionable company in itself, it was all too likely that he might be called upon to escort Anilee Mortimer, and there was time enough and more for that in his future.

With genuine curiosity, he inquired, "Do you solve every problem by running away?"

Haughtily, she retorted, "Certainly not! My parcel, please."

Lord Rutledge said pleasantly, "I think not. Not until I know what this is all about."

Pommy drew herself up to her full height, the top of her ringlets barely reaching to his shoulder. Dressed in her modest cloak, having been caught scandalously stealing out of the house in the night and disgracefully ready to brave the dangers of the city, nonetheless he had to admit her self-assurance was impressive.

In her most quelling manner and falling back on her training, she informed him, "I cannot perceive that my affairs can be of any interest to you. You will recall that we have not even been introduced."

His laugh rang heartily in the chilly air.

Alarmed, she scolded, "You'll wake everybody."

"You're right," he said in an altered voice. "We don't want interference, do we?"

He swooped on her and grabbed her wrist, firmly enough to discourage any hope of escaping, and they set off down the pavement.

When she could catch her breath, she gasped, "Where are you taking me?"

"Where you'll be safe," he said briefly, but he noticed her distress, half-running beside him, and slowed his pace.

To his home? she wondered. To some house of ill repute? With new visions of unnamed disaster in her mind, she faced bleakly the coil she had got herself into.

Justin Harcourt, for his part, could have allayed her fears. But as he grew sober, he became prey to serious misgivings. He was above all angry at the girl, unreasonably, for putting him into this situation, one that he could not control just yet, and disgusted with himself for succumbing even slightly to his need for one last irresponsible caper before the jaws of matrimony closed inexorably on him.

Not loosening his grip on her wrist, he almost dragged the source of all his present uncertainty into a dark and most likely sinister unknown, for all Pommy knew.

Nothing worse could happen now, she thought wretchedly, and at that moment the heavens opened and the storm was upon them.

3

The rain fell as though someone had upended a vast and full bucket over their heads. Pommy's cloak was soaked through in moments, and the sodden cloth of her gown wrapped itself around her legs. She stumbled and slipped to her knees. His grip on her wrist held her from sprawling on the pavement, but she felt a pain in her shoulder and cried out.

"Are you hurt?" he asked automatically. By the violet-edged illumination of a great stab of lightning, he saw her shake her head. But he also was provided with a clear view of the havoc the rain was wreaking on his captive. Her wet clothing molded itself to her body as though caressing it, and he noted her appearance with approval. But he also saw the misery in her face.

Her eyes, shadowed so he could not discern their color, seemed too large for the heart-shaped face. Her hood had fallen back when she stumbled, and her curls were plastered to her forehead. Rain streamed unhindered down her cheeks. She looked like a child beset by woes she could not run away from.

He was moved to gentleness.

He pulled her carefully inside his heavy cloak and put his arm around her, hugging her closely to him to give her what warmth he could, and they set out again, more slowly, heads bent against the rain.

To his relief, she made no move to escape. The rain had apparently dampened any resistance on her part. He matched his steps to hers, and they proceeded down Bruton Street, crossed Bond Street into Conduit Street, and turned left at the next corner.

"There's no shelter nearby, my dear," he said, thinking regretfully of the fire that without doubt warmed his own bachelor rooms, the entrance to which they had recently passed, "until we reach our destination."

A muffled voice within his cloak answered. "Your destination."

He chuckled. It would take more than a cloudburst to extinguish this lady's spirit. "There'll be a fire and something hot to drink in a few moments," he promised, hoping he spoke the truth.

They walked for what to Pommy seemed miles. In the darkness she had no idea where they were. Nothing looked familiar. They must be nearly to Gresham Street, she thought, and how could she get away from him to take the coach? Even the journey she was determined to make might well take her out of the frying pan, but also might drop her into the fire. She was not in the least sure of her grandmother's welcome at the end of her stage journey, since the dowager duchess did not know she was coming, nor had she to date expressed any willingness to become acquainted with her.

Pommy's thoughts refused to think about Grandmother, but concentrated with eagerness on hot fire and drink promised by this man she did not know, the amenities to appear in a place also unknown. She sneezed.

The street they were traversing debouched into a square, large houses in their own extensive grounds rising on all

sides. Memory stirred in Pommy. She had been taken by
Cousin Lydia to tea in one of these houses—they were in
Hanover Square.

All but one of the houses were dark, as befitted the
advanced hour of the night. But the mansion on the left was
ablaze with lights on the lower two floors. It was evident
that entertainment on a fairly large scale was drawing to a
close. She remembered hearing, as they walked in the rain,
the sound of carriage wheels and horses—a great many
carriages, she thought—coming from this direction.

Rutledge brought her up short at the edge of the square.
She glanced up at him and saw him clearly for the first time.
The subdued light coming from the house showed her rather
undistinguished features, save for a cleft chin, heavy eyebrows, and from what she could see, a mouth that she knew
could be possessive and, perhaps, sensitive. Altogether,
she concluded, a face that matched his high-handed
ways.

His lips were just now compressed into a thin line, having
just emitted a regrettably strong curse. He seemed to have
forgotten Pommy and removed his restraining arm from her.
She had no inclination to run away.

"What did you say?"

"Never mind. I did not speak for your ears. But I just
recalled that I was to be in attendance at that party that is
just now breaking up, and I completely forgot it."

A lone carriage now appeared at the opposite side of the
square and moved slowly to stop in front of the great house.
A footman dropped from the seat and ran to open the carriage
door in readiness for the home-going passengers. There was
an obvious stir from inside the house. The guests, possibly
the last of the evening, were on the verge of departure.

"Come on," Lord Rutledge said in a decisive whisper,
and dragged her after him to the side lawn nearest them. "If

we can get to the back before they come out, we may count ourselves fortunate.''

"Where are we going?'' Pommy demanded, pulling back. A hot fire and a warm drink were not, in her experience, to be found in soaking shrubbery in a dark garden.

"Quiet!''

But they were not to reach their goal at the moment. As they drew abreast of the front entrance, the door opened wide and light streamed out across the steps and onto the carriage in the street. More to the point, the glow of an enormous number of wax candles illuminated the section of the garden where Lord Rutledge and Pommy stood.

"Quick!''

To her surprise he pulled her toward the house, not away, and into the shrubbery beside the front steps. In their dark garments, they were effectively concealed in the shadows.

Pommy considered that she had spent the greater part of her recent life crouched under dripping bushes. At least, she amended, to be truthful, it was only these bushes that dripped. Nonetheless, the evening had not turned out quite as she had planned it.

She turned to speak to her companion, but he, most ungallantly, shoved her head down onto her knees. "They'll see you,'' he whispered savagely. "Keep your head down.''

He was a tyrant and an obnoxious interferer, and his fingers on the back of her neck were light. Now was the time to get away from him, if ever there was one.

Or she could scream. Help was certainly at hand.

But screaming meant discovery, and that meant scandal. Besides, she was becoming interested in what was going on here.

She could hear nothing to the point—only the rainwater running in the gutters, now that it had almost stopped, and the impatient jingling of harness.

Her companion made as if to rise, but there was a sudden stir on the steps and he subsided. Two ladies and a man appeared on the threshold, clearly saying farewell to their hostess. The butler, his back to the two in concealment, held the door for the departing guests.

"Do you know them?" she whispered.

"To my sorrow, I do."

One of the two ladies was younger than the others, likely a daughter with her parents. The young lady was not tall, and was slightly built. Her hair, in the light the color of a new-minted coin, lay in flat curls atop her head.

Pommy took an instant dislike to her, for no reason save that the young lady was wrapped in furs and was descending the steps now to a warm carriage, while she herself would never be dry or warm again.

One of the three flung a last word over her shoulder to the elegant lady who stood in the doorway. "We shall see you at Lisle Court, then?"

"Of course," came the lilting voice of the unseen hostess. That voice . . . Somewhere Pommy thought she had heard it before. "We're all looking forward so much to the visit."

Pommy may not have been brought into London society, but she had much experience in the ways of the world in Bedfordshire. The words she heard spoken were cordial. But Pommy was at once convinced that the ladies were far from bosom friends.

The lady of the house stepped back into her house, and the butler, seemingly testing the night air, said in a voice that did not carry far, "The side door to the conservatory is not locked, my lord."

No sooner had the butler closed the door, leaving the surroundings of the house in darkness, than Rutledge moved. He pulled Pommy after him around the side of the house. The lawn was broad and long. At the far end of the expanse she could now see the outlines of a conservatory against the clearing sky.

The rain was over. Raindrops pattered down from time to time as a light breeze shook the wet leaves overhead.

They reached the conservatory. To be with her captor in the open, where with a little luck she could escape him, was one thing, but to be within walls, especially walls whose owner was a mystery to her, was quite another.

"Whose house is this?" she demanded.

He did not answer. He seemed to be familiar with their surroundings, for he went directly to the door mentioned by the butler, and opened it. She pulled away on the threshold.

The greenhouse was large, filled with a great many splendid plants, each of some size. Lights were placed discreetly among the foliage, furnishing many shadowy recesses alluring to flirtatiously inclined couples. Pommy and her captor ignored their surroundings.

Feeling braver in the light, Pommy mutinied. "I'm not going a step further with you without an explanation."

Rutledge, tried beyond endurance, finally lost his temper. He was suffering from guilt over the part he had played this night with this unknown girl, knowing she was gently born, and he had handled her as though she were a servant—had even kissed her. His conscience also pointed out that he had forgotten the party his sister had given to honor his intended fiancée and her parents. Knowing this unwanted marriage lay inexorably in his path, his only recourse had been to get excessively foxed, and look what that had led to.

His next step did not alleviate the situation.

He glared at the prize he had brought all the way from Berkeley Square, and told her, "You'll do as I say. Get through that door, or I'll sling you over my shoulder and carry you."

She glared back at him, rebellious to the end. But she

changed her mind quickly when he advanced on her with determination. She glanced for help at the butler standing in the door leading to the interior of the house, but his impassive gaze was fixed on a point somewhere beyond her left shoulder.

Quickly Pommy stepped through the door.

She found herself in a narrow hallway, covered with black and white tiles. This house, whomever it belonged to, was well kept, for the pleasantly domestic aroma of beeswax was strong.

"This way, my lord," urged the butler. "I suggest the small sitting room at the back of the house would be most private."

Pommy and her captor followed the servant, and shortly were ushered into a casually comfortable room. Noticing details because she did not want to think about the larger aspects of her present situation, she supposed this charming room to be a private retreat for the mistress of the house. Wide, undraped windows looked out on darkness, probably an enclosed garden. On the wall opposite, a small fire crackled on a large hearth, and comfortable-looking chairs were placed in small friendly groupings around the room.

Pommy, rubbing her wrist, moved to the windows. Her captor came to stand beside her, fearful, perhaps, she would try to escape by crashing through the windows. Again she was aware, too aware, of his scent, soap mingled with tobacco and a touch of wine. With a deliberate effort, she blotted out the memory of the touch of his lips on hers. He was a villain, an abductor, a brute, and deserved no consideration from her. It would not be wonderful if she found her wrist covered with blood from the wounds made by his fingers as he dragged her through the streets of London, like a Roman triumphal procession.

She turned toward him, a few wounding words of her own

on her tongue, but he was paying no heed to her. He was in consultation with the butler, whom he seemed to know well.

"I will inform Lady Playre of your arrival, my lord," said the butler as calmly as though he were accustomed daily to gentlemen arriving by a side door, dragging women behind them.

"Thank you, Blaise. By the way, there is no need, I think, to inform his lordship of our arrival."

"Just so, my lord."

Blaise built up the fire before closing the door firmly behind him, leaving Pommy and Lord Rutledge alone. Justin had leisure now to contemplate his recent sins. In the firelight, the lady appeared to no better advantage than she had standing in the middle of Conduit Street streaming with rain.

Now he could see that she was white with weariness. Dark circles under her eyes made them seem even larger. And her hair . . . the lamplight touched it as though with a flame. He felt an unaccustomed stab of guilt.

Good God, what had he done this night?

"You'll be better out of those wet clothes," he said at last.

Pommy, neatly provided with an excuse to vent her turbulent emotions, demanded, "Just how shall I do that? You have the total of my possessions in that parcel you stole from me, and I don't even know your name. You've spoiled everything, and I dare not even think how my life is ruined."

He had expected tears and pleadings, but he had not expected her to break down, as she now did, into such bitter sobs. She moved blindly to a cushioned chair near the fire, but at the last moment remembered her damp skirts and instead stood on the hearth, warming herself on the dying embers of the fire. She hid her face in her hands and refused to say any more. He watched her helplessly.

* * *

The butler's mission to find Lady Playre ran into difficulty immediately. Just outside the door, his master approached from the front of the house.

"Blaise, did you notice whether I left my folio of papers in the sitting room?"

"My lord," Blaise said hastily, keeping his place before the door he had just closed. "I believe I saw it in the library. I shall bring it to you upstairs."

"No, I remember now," said Lord Playre. "I was working on them here this afternoon." Brought up short by his butler's immobility, he added, "What the devil's the matter with you, Blaise? Either open the door or get out of my way, you fool."

There was nothing for it but for Blaise to step aside, open the door for his master, and wait for the expected explosion. On second thought, the wiser course—and the one which he swiftly followed—was to remove himself from the vicinity and inform Lady Playre of the arrival of her brother.

Gervase Quentin, Lord Playre, entering a room he thought empty, was startled to find his brother-in-law standing in the middle, glaring at him with a far-from-cordial expression.

"Rutledge," exclaimed Gervase, taken aback, "what are you doing here at this hour? Too late for the party. Everybody's gone. Caroline was in quite a taking when you didn't show up. You know she can't stand Miss Mortimer above half, and the party was for you, after all—"

He broke off abruptly when his eyes fell on the slender young figure, face covered by her hands, dripping water onto the hearth rug. Bewildered by the sight of what he considered a waif off the streets, he began, as he did when moved, to sputter.

"Good God, Justin! Now you've gone too far. No objection to your doxy, of course, although I think you could do better than that wisp of a thing. But to bring her here to your sister's! Through the back door, as I suppose, while your betrothed is departing from the front. Such effrontery. I don't blame you in the least, Justin, and I've told you this before, for shying away from that . . . Shouldn't say it, I know, but I cannot fathom what your sister will have to say."

They were not left long in the dark on that head.

From the doorway, quietly opened by Blaise, spoke Lady Playre. "Say about what, Gervase?"

The faces turned toward her reflected a variety of moods. Her husband threw up his hands, clearly resigned to the worst. Her brother's expression was eager and full of hope, since he had cast Caroline in the role of rescuer. The dim figure silhouetted against the firelight told Lady Playre nothing.

Gervase struggled to make the best of what he considered a very shabby situation. "No need to bother you, m'dear. You must be fagged to death after the party—"

Justin, ignoring his brother-in-law, interrupted hastily. "I can explain, Caroline. Indeed, I must explain."

Caroline Quentin, Lady Playre, looked with commendable calm and some amusement upon her only brother, of whom she was excessively fond. "I do hope you have a tale to tell me, Justin. I shall of course want to know why you avoided my party tonight. Later will do."

"Caroline . . ." began her husband.

She ignored him. "Justin, don't tell me you are now taking to rescuing climbing boys?" She regarded the thin figure at the fire. "Perhaps too tall. Crossing sweeps, then?"

Gervase was not to be silenced. "Can't you use your eyes? It's a female. I told him he shouldn't bring his bit of fluff here, of all places."

Justin sent a quelling glance at Lord Playre. "Quiet, Gervase, and you too, Caroline. Be quiet and listen to me."

Pommy had been sunk in wretchedness. She had extended

her courage to the breaking point simply by deciding to brave whatever storms her grandmother might bring down around her head. To steal out in the night was so scandalous she refused to consider the consequences. But she would have made it, she really would! Except for the untimely interference of this stranger, she would now be at the coaching inn, waiting for the start to Middlesex in the morning.

Wet and cold, she could feel her toes squishing in her sodden boots—ruined, of course. She had been only minimally aware of her surroundings, until she caught the altered note in Justin's voice. Afraid of what he was going to say and yet knowing she could do nothing to prevent him, she looked up quickly. At that moment the lamplight fell full on her face.

Caroline was standing at the right place to catch the movement, and could see clearly the features of the figure at the hearth.

She drew a quick, sharp breath. Climbing boy? Crossing sweep? Doxy? Recognition leapt in her eyes.

Pommy, paying attention to her surroundings finally, remembered to whom the half-familiar voice belonged. She was safe. Feeling now that something was required of her, she took a step forward. Her hands went out in a moving little gesture. "Lady Playre—"

Lady Playre, her voice filled with horror, stepped back. "Good God, Justin," she breathed, unconsciously echoing her brother, "what have you done?"

4

What had he done?

Justin looked from his sister to the young lady and back.

He read in Caroline's eyes the unsettling conviction that the pit he had dug for himself yawned ominously at his feet.

"You have brought here—under duress, I should imagine—a young lady . . ." Curiosity struck Caroline. "How on earth did you come across her?" She turned to Pommy. "I cannot conceive any way your path could have crossed my brother's."

Aghast, Justin exclaimed, "You know her? You can't. Caroline, you are getting back at me—in a very childish fashion, I must say—for missing your party. You simply cannot be acquainted with her. I caught her absconding with someone's silver."

"A thief? Do be serious."

Justin had to cling to the premise that his captive was a criminal. Otherwise, scandal breathed down his neck.

"Probably well-known at Newgate," he insisted stoutly, "under the name of Lady Jane, to match her acquired ways."

Nonetheless, his spirits were sinking ever lower with each word his sister spoke. His words rang hollowly in his ears. He knew he spoke trumpery. It was lowering indeed to

realize he had been mistaken, it seemed, in every conclusion
he had drawn.

"You couldn't have," said Lady Playre flatly. "This lady
you have so unceremoniously brought in circumstances I can
only refer to as outrageous is Pommy Fiske."

"Pommy?" echoed Justin, grasping at straws. "Impossible. There is no such name as Pommy."

"If you paid attention to what is going on around you, I
have mentioned Miss Fiske more than once."

Gervase, being thoroughly bewildered by events taking
place before him, events that baffled explanation, weighed
in heavily. "Caroline, if you know this young lady, why is
she here with Justin?"

"I haven't the faintest idea, my love. But Miss Fiske,"
she added, addressing Pommy for the first time, "you do
recall we met at tea at Lady Bryce's across the square?"

"Yes, Lady Playre, I do remember you," Pommy said
with dignity. "I regret that we meet again under such
questionable circumstances, but pray believe me, it is none
of my doing." She sent a smoldering glance toward Justin.

Lord Rutledge wondered how he could ever have thought
her a maidservant or, even more incredible, a footman.

"Then, what, Miss Pommy Fiske," Justin said sternly,
"were you doing climbing out of a house in the dead of night
dressed like a—dressed like *that*?"

"I was simply traveling to my grandmother's home," she
said with dignity.

"In the night? And with only that foolish parcel—wrapped
in a shawl!—as luggage? I think not."

"Quiet, Justin," Caroline said. Thoughtfully, she eyed
Pommy. "Somehow you do not look the same as before."

"For one thing," Justin put in, "she needs dry clothes
or she'll come down with lung congestion." Unnecessarily,
he explained, "We got caught in the storm."

"For another thing," said Caroline, ignoring her brother, "your dress. The last time I saw you you were wearing an afternoon gown of Pomona green."

"I could hardly wear that on the stage," Pommy explained earnestly.

Gervase could be heard muttering, "The stage? An actress? Good God, what next?"

"No, Lord Playre. I am not an actress. While I know it is not the thing," she told him earnestly, "to travel by public coach, I had no choice."

It had been a long time since Pommy had heard a sympathetic voice. Lady Playre had been kind at Lady Bryce's tea, and she turned to her. "When I left, I thought I should take only the things that are mine. Although I suppose they all were, since I think my father paid for them. But the pearls are mine, from my mother." She gestured toward the shapeless bundle lying where Justin had dropped it on a table. "My jewel case is in that."

Belatedly, Lady Playre recalled her duty. "Just a moment . . ."

She stepped to the door, and Pommy could hear her speaking to the butler, who had undoubtedly, in the way of butlers, been listening just outside the door. Pommy did not even try to catch the words, for she was tired, wet, disappointed, and to be honest, very anxious about her future, which was at the moment in the hands of these strangers.

She knew she had behaved badly this night. Cousin Lydia had pointed out her faults over and over again. "Such a hoyden, no one will offer for you. I doubt it is worthwhile to bring you into society at all . . . Such shabby behavior." Pommy could not recall any example of outrageous behavior, at least behavior that would cause eyebrows to lift in Bedfordshire, where she had lived all her life. Sometimes she thought darkly that Cousin Lydia was crying wolf for reasons Pommy could not even guess.

But Cousin Lydia had told her sufficiently often that she had begun to believe her, "Such a disappointment to your father, and how I shall ever get you wed I do not know. Only one chance for you, my girl, in spite of your fortune. You're lucky that my Frederick has an eye for you." She had heard it all, and more than once.

When Caroline came back into the room, she said, "Your room will be ready directly, and you can get out of those wet clothes. We are much of a size and I think I can find something to fit. Blaise will send you up something to eat. But tell me—I confess that I am curious—how did you plan to get to your grandmother's? And, by the way, which grandmother?"

"I have only one," said Pommy. "I never knew Grandmother Fiske. Truthfully, I do not know my other grandmother, but I hope . . . I believe . . . that is, she must take me in."

"Whyever should she not?" Justin wondered.

"Because she and my father . . . Oh, what difference does it make to you anyway." Pommy's good nature had suffered much in the last hour. "I shall have to marry that awful Frederick, and all anybody can do is ask st-stupid questions!"

"My dear child!" Lady Playre's voice was warm and her arm went swiftly around Pommy's damp shoulders. "I promise you, you shall not marry Frederick—tonight, at any rate. Justin, I wish you will go home, and let me deal—"

Gervase had held his tongue long enough. There were things going on in his own house that he did not understand. He had every faith in his wife's ability to deal, as she said, but still, a man ought to know what is going on.

"My dear, it seems to me that the problem, whatever it

is, is your brother's. I have never thought Rutledge incompetent you know—''

"Thank you," Justin said gravely.

"But I don't understand why somebody's granddaughter doesn't want to marry Frederick and why"—here Gervase's voice rose querulously—"Justin got mixed up in it. After all, he's betrothed to Miss Mortimer."

And what she would say to the point, Justin dreaded to think. He spoke in mollifying tones. "Gervase, I had to bring Miss Fiske here."

"Why not leave her where she was?"

"I couldn't abandon her, and there was no place else."

"No place?"

"Not after I deceived the watch."

"Deceived—"

"Gervase," his wife said, "for goodness' sake be quiet for a moment. Miss Fiske must be put to bed. Gervase, you must see there is nothing else to do?"

Her husband breathed heavily for a moment and then agreed. "Well, it's too late to do anything tonight. We can send her back in the morning."

Pommy had not been following the conversation closely. Into her dreams of hot drink and warm bed dropped words that affected her. "Back? Oh, no, you cannot send me back to her."

"But you must go somewhere," Caroline said gently. "Where, then?"

Belatedly, Pommy became prudent. She did not wish to make the world privy to all her plans of escape from London. Public stage she had mentioned, and grandmother as well, and both without proper caution. Those plans had been interrupted, but only deferred, not canceled. She suspected, rightly, that she was dealing with people with the power to thwart her. Though she had felt comfortable with Lady Playre at the first, yet Pommy was convinced that her involuntary hostess lived by the set of rules current in London, and in society in general, the same rules that seemed designed to put her into a wretched marriage and a miserable life.

Everything had gone awry for her since she was brought to London by an uncaring parent. She was on her own and she intended to keep things that way. If they were to think she had given up her fixed plan, she might yet get away safely.

The fire felt warm and comforting on her back, and her dress was nearly dry. She knew they were waiting for her answer, but she seemed unable to speak.

She looked at Lord Playre, who intended to send her back to Cousin Lydia and Frederick. She glanced at Lady Playre, who was regarding her with bright, curious eyes. Perhaps Pommy had already told Caroline too much.

She glanced at Justin, her nemesis, who had interfered so decisively in her life and for whom she entertained a growing dislike.

Because of the warmth of the room after her walk in the rain, or perhaps because she had been too distressed all day to eat, the faces around her began to blur and she slid to the floor in a faint.

Later, after Pommy had been forced to eat some hot soup and drink a glass of warm milk and been put to bed in one of Caroline's night robes, the Playres and Justin gathered again in the back sitting room.

"You know," said Caroline thoughtfully, "as a family, we talk too much. That poor child, shivering in her wet clothes and probably starving, and we went on and on thinking what to do with her tomorrow. That is, I suppose I mean today."

"I don't understand," Gervase said slowly. "From what

you said, I could almost believe you picked the girl up on the street. But if she's a lady, then that is impossible.''

The time had come, Justin thought, to explain everything.

"First I need to apologize, Caroline. Your party for Anilee went right out of my head.''

"And I wish the girl herself would do so,'' muttered Caroline, but softly enough so that Justin did not hear. In a firmer voice she added, "So, instead you went to Watier's?''

"Brooks's. And drank more than usual.''

"Come out ahead?'' Gervase asked. Justin nodded. "Gave the money away, I suppose. Well, go on.''

"And when I got to Berkeley Square, headed for my room, here was this person climbing down some kind of trellis, I suppose it was, from the terrace. What would you think, Gervase?''

"I'd think I was so drunk I had hallucinations,'' his brother-in-law said promptly.

"I thought she was a footman stealing the silver, truly I did,'' Justin said bluntly. He told the rest of the story, except for the few moments when he had thought she was merely a maidservant and therefore to be embraced, even kissed thoroughly, if he wished.

After he fell silent, Caroline said, "So, you brought her here, after you recognized her.''

"I didn't recognize her. How could I? I have never seen her before. Only I could tell finally by her voice that she was no servant. But why didn't she tell me who she was? I gave her sufficient opportunity.''

"Pride possibly, dear brother. Do you know who she really is?''

Promptly he said, "Pommy Fiske. You said so. On the understanding, of course, that Pommy is a real name.''

"Her grandmother, dear brother, is the dowager Duchess of Woodburn. She lives next to our country place—that is, yours now, of course. You surely remember the duchess?''

"Certainly I do. She's your godmother.''

Gervase said, surprised, "I thought she was dead.''

"This girl is her granddaughter? I didn't know she had any family at all.''

"She had a daughter who married, as our mother said, to disoblige her. Married Sir Arthur Fiske.''

"Now, I know something about that man,'' Gervase said, searching his memory. "Does something with Greek statues, doesn't he?''

Caroline nodded. "His wife died in childbirth and he was left with Pommy.'' She caught Justin's eye. "I know Pommy is not an ordinary name. The duchess told me that he had planned to name all his daughters after the Muses, but since Pommy was the first and only one, he had her christened Melpomene, after the Muse of Tragedy.''

"Thank God,'' Justin said, shuddering, "there was just the one. Nine muses storming London is not to be thought of.''

"But where is she from? And what is she doing in London?'' Gervase added peevishly. "And stealing the silver? No, Justin, you were too foxed to think. That little parcel there couldn't hold even a tray.''

"As she pointed out,'' Justin said ruefully, "but it was too late then. I could not leave the girl alone in the street in the middle of the night.''

"You don't think she stole anything, do you?'' asked Caroline, watching him closely.

Justin turned away. In a muffled voice he said, "I was just so damned bored!''

Gervase said, "I suppose she came to town for the Season, you know. I heard that Sir Arthur had gone to Greece. Hope he's not killed there. The Turks are causing trouble again.''

Justin was pursuing his own train of thought. "Who is this Frederick that she is to marry?"

"I ought to know, but I can't think. Do you realize it is past two o'clock? And I've been on my feet all day."

"Why doesn't her grandmother have her while her father is out of the country?" Gervase asked.

"Oh, didn't I tell that? The duchess was so furious when her daughter—Julia, her name was—married this Fiske person that she cast her out. Never even turned over the family jewels that were part of Julia's dowry. Julia's husband was so furious he wouldn't let the duchess visit them. She may not ever have seen Pommy."

"And so this poor thing," Justin said, outraged, "was running away to her?"

"What would you have her do, under the circumstances?" Gervase said, in a voice designed to end discussion, "What she is told to do."

Caroline flared up. "You heard what she thought of this Frederick. You think she should be forced to marry him?"

Justin pointed out, "No one is forced to marry these days."

"Her guardians," Gervase said, "know what is best for her."

Justin, weary and somehow deflated as the excitement of the evening wore down, said, "Well, I wash my hands of her."

With a sister's frankness, Lady Playre said, "Of course you do. How typical. Get yourself into a coil and then dump your problems on someone else."

Justin, justifiably indignant, said, "Not all of them. After all, I do not complain about . . ." Too late, he saw the direction his thoughts were taking. The biggest coil he had ever been in, thanks to overly zealous parents, both his and Miss Mortimer's, was his compact to wed a young lady whom he did not love, but whom he was convinced he would actively dislike. And he was not asking his sister to pull those chestnuts out of the fire.

Quickly, Justin suggested, "We'll all think more clearly in the morning."

After Lord Rutledge departed, Gervase eyed his wife with suspicion. He had known her long and well, and now he demanded, "What are you scheming, my dear?"

Apparently at a tangent, she said, "Did you notice, he called her poor thing?"

"Yes. And if you mean our unexpected guest, the description is accurate enough."

"I suppose you wouldn't see the significance of it. But it's the first sign of humanity I've seen in him for two years, and I am excessively glad to hear it."

Gervase was uneasy. "No tricks now."

In an innocent voice, she said, "Of course not, darling. Just because I cannot abide Anilee—"

"I wish you not to interfere in your brother's business. He will not thank you for it."

Virtuously, she reassured him. "Believe me, Gervase, I do know what is the proper thing to do."

Lord Playre put the screen in place before the fire. Offering his arm as they ascended the stairs to bed, he said gloomily, "That gives me no comfort whatever."

5

Pommy woke to a new day, and a giddy sense of displacement. After some weeks, she had become accustomed though not resigned to waking in her cousin's rented house in Berkeley Square. In her bedroom there, the morning light picked out a ceiling made of plaster medallions in the Italian fashion.

But this ceiling overhead now was none of hers, she decided as she lay still and let her eyes explore. She had never seen this room before, and her memory provided, at least for the moment, no hint of where she was or how she had got here.

Carefully turning her head, she saw what appeared to be a bedroom furnished in quite the first order. Curtains in a patterned kind of India cloth, cheerful with scarlet and blue, hung at the windows, and a pair of chairs flanking the hearth were covered to match. The floor, too, was covered by a lustrous carpet of an unfamiliar pattern. Pommy was puzzled to realize she had stood on that very carpet, and recently, too.

At some time she had stood with bare feet on this carpet, and memory came back in a rush. Last night . . . the shaky trellis . . . the obnoxious gentleman who brought her here.

She quickly got out of bed. Surprised, she saw she was

wearing a night shift strange to her. Somebody, undoubtedly a maid, had undressed her and put her to bed.

But where were her own clothes? The bedroom was nicely, even lavishly furnished, save in the crucial matter of clothes.

Lady Playre had seemed nice last night. But the fact was, Pommy believed, she was at this very moment a prisoner in a supposedly respectable mansion in Hanover Square. How could decent persons bring her here and remove her clothes?

A slight tap at the door and her overnight hostess bustled in. Pommy's doubts were answered. Lady Playre carried Pommy's clothes over her arm.

"Good morning, my dear. Your clothes have been cleaned and are as good as new. Though I do not scruple to tell you that they were not particularly elegant at the start. Why on earth did you choose such totally undistinguished garments?" She dropped the offending clothing on a chair and turned to Miss Fiske.

Pommy explained. "I left with my own things, those I brought with me from home. You must know that in the country no one dresses in the height of fashion. I did not know precisely how one dresses for the public stage, but I did not think I could take my trunks along."

"I should think not."

"So I left all my new gowns behind."

"Well, if that green gown you wore at Lady Playre's is an example, I commend your good sense in leaving them. My dear, I must apologize for being so dim-witted last evening. I knew who you were and where we had met, but there was such a crush at Lady Bryce's, and I did not stay long. I did not realize that Lady Derwent was your father's cousin. Of course that is where you are staying in London."

Dutifully, Pommy said, "She has been very good to me."

Lady Playre was sufficiently shrewd to give that remark the credibility it deserved. "That, of course, is why my brother found you running away." She held up Pommy's gray gown. "No wonder he thought you were a thief."

"He didn't even ask. Of course, I dared not speak, lest he realize I was not a maidservant. But why did he have to interfere?"

Caroline, in whom the germ of an idea had appeared last evening and had not died overnight, asked with a fine artless air, "What do you think of my brother?"

Without hesitation, Pommy obliged. "He is the most high-handed person I have ever met. He is so full of himself. He thinks he is the only one who knows what is best—for everybody. And he does not listen. He could have let me go half a dozen times last night."

Satisfied with her guest's hotly unfavorable opinion of her brother, Lady Playre changed the subject. Dislike can so easily turn around and show the face of love. Had Pommy been indifferent, Caroline would have been disappointed.

"Let us have breakfast," she said, "and I shall tell you that I have written this morning to Lady Derwent. I am sorry, Pommy, but you see that I must have done so."

"You're no better . . ." Pommy stopped short. "I do beg your pardon, Lady Playre—"

"Please call me Caroline."

"But I should like to have been consulted on a matter so near to me. I do not intend to go back to Cousin Lydia's. She'll have an excuse now to keep me prisoner until I marry Frederick."

"Surely not."

Believe her or not, thought Pommy, she had overheard what she had not been meant to hear. She simply shrugged her shoulders. "I wish you had not told her where I am."

"But I had to. She could not be left to worry about you," Lady Playre explained.

"Believe me, she will not care. I doubt if she would miss me any time before noon."

"Who is this Frederick who figured so large in your thoughts last night?"

"Frederick Watters," Pommy said.

"I do not remember meeting him."

"No doubt you have not. He does not go about much in society, and I believe he prefers the sporting circles, as he calls them. He is Cousin Lydia's son from her first husband. I never knew him, and of course he is dead long since. So is her second husband. I scarcely knew her before my father brought me here."

"And Frederick wishes to marry you?"

"Cousin Lydia wishes him to. For the money, I suppose. I believe there is quite a bit of it."

"And you do not wish it?"

"I don't wish to marry anyone, Lady Playre—"

"Call me Caroline."

"Caroline. My father may not have any affection for me, but he does see that the proper things are done for me. I think he may be afraid of my grandmother. But I do know my father wished me to have a Season for the purpose of making a match for me. But now I won't have the Season and I will have to marry anyway." She was silent for a moment. Then she burst out, "My grandmother is my only hope."

Lady Playre, remembering certain conversations with the dowager duchess on the subject of her son-in-law, held a dark view of an open-armed welcome at Edgecumbe Manor in Middlesex.

"But do you not think that the duchess will be better pleased if you write to her first?"

"You know her? I did not tell you her name, did I?"

"No, but you must know that she is my godmother. After

all, Justin and I grew up at Lisle Court, next neighbors to the duchess.''

Pommy retreated into stubbornness. "I won't face Cousin Lydia.''

Briskly, Caroline said, "You will have to someday. But most likely, not today, for I should be gravely mistaken if Lady Derwent, who is not known for her energy, does more than acknowledge my note for the moment.''

She was proven wrong almost at once when Blaise announced the arrival of Lady Derwent and Mr. Watters.

"So soon? I would not have thought it.'' She saw with a start that Pommy had paled and her eyes were anxious.

Lady Playre took a sudden decision. "Do you stay here,'' she said, rising. "I should be glad were you to stay here with me as long as you like.'' Recklessly, she added, "You need not go home with them. I'll think of something. But you stay here, and do not even move.''

Left alone, Pommy gave way to her darkest apprehensions. Three months since her entire orderly life had been turned upside down. She had scarcely ever been away from her father's estate in Bedfordshire. From time to time her father had departed on one or another of his expeditions to Greece, or to Oxford, or even to London, and never had he suggested that Pommy accompany him. But to give him credit, he had seen that her education was of the best. "The furnishings of the mind will stay when all else is gone,'' he said quite often.

And besides education, he had employed an expensive governess to teach Pommy how to make her way in society. After all, she was a duke's granddaughter and that witch of a mother-in-law of his would never find opportunity to accuse him of a shabby upbringing.

Pommy, therefore, had believed that she would be able

to hold her own in London society, and while she had done
nothing very wrong, she thought, her father's Cousin Lydia
had not hidden her shock at Pommy's indiscretions.

It was not until she had overheard Lydia Derwent and her
dreary son, Frederick, conversing in Lady Derwent's sitting
room that she began to understand exactly what she had to
look forward to, not just in London, but for the rest of her
life. And since she knew she could not count on her father
to rescue her—after all, he must now be digging happily on
a sun-drenched island in the Aegean—she felt she had no
recourse but flight.

And at this moment, she should have been on the stage
to Middlesex, to a grandmother she did not know and who
did not want even to know her.

Even her attempt at escape had gone for naught, thanks
to the excessively interfering Lord Rutledge. What a cruel
turn of fate had brought him to the square at the wrong time!
And to cap it all, she was now in the hands of people who
cared enough about her to see that she was safe—but not
happy.

It was all Lord Rutledge's fault.

However, one thing she was determined upon: she would
never marry Frederick, who wanted her fortune to pay off
his gambling debts and had not the slightest wish to take her
along with the money.

And if her father had agreed to this marriage, as Cousin
Lydia had told her, then it was the cruelest thing he had ever
done to her.

Lady Playre had told her to stay in her room until she
returned. But Pommy suddenly realized that it had been a
long time since Caroline had gone down to speak to Lady
Derwent. What could be happening?

Pommy considered that the discussion in the salon below
concerned her nearly, and while strictures on eavesdropping

were strong, yet Pommy felt justified in trying at least to learn whether the exchange of views was amicable. If Lady Playre were to betray her, then she had every right to know.

She left her room quietly and stole to the head of the stairway. She had not seen this part of the house, since Blaise had brought them in through the conservatory the night before. She stood for a moment, getting her bearings. The stairs led down into a large foyer. At the far end was the front entrance, and on either side were doors leading to, she supposed, salons and dining rooms of various styles.

No servant was on duty and there was no indication of which room held Lady Playre and Lady Derwent.

Listening, she soon heard voices, but she could not distinguish words. Perhaps if she descended a few steps . . .

By the time she was able to catch a few words—especially Cousin Lydia's, since her voice tended to rise when she was moved—Pommy was almost at the bottom of the stairs.

She could hear quite well and did not like what she heard.

Lydia Derwent had become suspicious. "I still do not understand, Lady Playre, just how my young cousin arrived here from Berkeley Square. Hanover Square, of course, is quite some distance to walk, and I feel someone must have brought her here."

"How she arrived is nothing to the point," said Caroline.

"I think it is most important. Certainly the child would know it is most unacceptable to leave the house of her guardian for any reason. She must have been abducted."

Here Frederick interrupted. "If she's caused a scandal, then of course my mother cannot take her back."

Lady Playre said, tightly, "She was not seduced."

Young Mr. Watters doggedly followed his train of thought. "No one will recognize her socially if she's been ruined. I would not wish to marry her myself."

Lady Derwent hurried to undo the damage. "Of course,

we do not think she had been ruined. Frederick, you are talking nonsense. You will remember that the announcement of your betrothal has gone to the *Gazette*."

Caroline was shocked. "Then you are not bringing the girl out?"

"It is totally out of the question. She is such a hoyden, accustomed to rural society of a kind I shudder to think of. No, much as her father might wish it, I consider it best not to humiliate the girl. She would be laughed at for months."

"She seems to me," Lady Playre objected, "to be particularly well-mannered. I should have no hesitation in sponsoring her myself."

Lady Derwent was alarmed. Lady Playre's social standing was impeccable. It would not do for her to seize the reins, for Pommy, abroad on the social scene, would be able to choose among at least several eligible suitors. It was to Frederick's advantage, and his mother's, to keep her from recognizing her own value.

"Well," she said crossly, "you will not have the opportunity. My son is anxious to be wed—"

Lady Playre's tolerance was not her strong point. In fact, it was nearly nonexistent. She had held her tongue throughout this entire sordid interview, and she told herself, she need only endure for another five minutes and this loathsome woman and her repulsive son would be out of her house.

It was not to be.

"Anxious to be wed? Or to get control of Pommy's money?" Caroline said. "Does her father know your plans? I know Lady Bryce told me—the day we met at tea there—that Sir Arthur wished her to be introduced to society."

Pommy was so intent on the conversation that she edged closer and closer, and when Blaise came upon her, she was standing in the middle of the foyer. The butler was an intelligent man and far better informed along certain lines than were his employers. He was privy to a large fund of servants' gossip that covered most of the fashionable West End of London, and while his information about the newest guest in the house was scanty, he suspected that Lord Rutledge, of whom he approved, had more than a passing interest in her. Besides, Blaise himself considered her a taking little thing.

In a moment he had established her behind the baize door, left ajar, at the back of the foyer. "The visitors will be leaving soon, miss," Blaise told her. She nodded understanding. He had wished her to be out of the way when Lady Derwent and her son passed through the foyer.

At this moment Justin, having seen the Derwent carriage before his sister's door and giving himself a two-block walk to avoid coming in the front entrance, arrived at the conservatory door. For a change, he was feeling quite cheerful. He had awakened that morning with anticipation. He had found in Miss Fiske's dilemma something to interest him, a puzzle to alleviate his usual state of ennui. Now he had come to see what the morning had brought.

He was intercepted at the inner conservatory door by the butler. "You will not wish to interrupt Lady Playre, who is receiving callers in the small salon. Please to come this way, my lord."

In a moment, Justin found himself beside Pommy, behind the baize door, clearly eavesdropping. Disapproving, he was about to scold her, but she scowled at him, put an admonishing finger to her lips, and quite shamelessly leaned forward the better to hear.

In a moment, he was caught by the proceedings as they unfolded.

Lady Derwent's voice came clearly through the salon door, purposely left open by Blaise. "We will take her home now. Perhaps it is not too late. We may be able to avert scandal when she is once again under the roof where her father placed her.''

Lady Playre was angry. Her tolerance had vanished. She said regally, ''No scandal can touch her in my house. You do not realize that the child is welcome to come to me at any time. You must know that Pommy's grandmother is also my godmother, so I know quite well who she is.''

For the first time there appeared a note of uneasiness in Lady Derwent's voice. ''The girl's grandmother will have nothing to do with her.'' Never one with a high regard for truth, she cast it off altogether. ''Her grace did refuse to take her while her father is out of the country. And Pommy needn't try to win her over, because her sentiments are well-known.''

''Not to me,'' retorted Caroline.

But Pommy did not hear any more. Tears welled up in her eyes and she felt a clean handkerchief thrust into her hands. Justin automatically gathered her close to him and held her while she cried.

He was outraged at the calm arrogance with which this woman and her son had taken over the future of this girl without so much as even a token request for her agreement. He could not believe even the eccentric Sir Arthur would throw his daughter to the wolves with such callousness.

Pommy pulled away from Justin and listened again.

Lady Derwent was in the foyer now, taking her leave. ''I shall send my son for her in the morning, since you tell me your doctor wishes her to remain quiet today. She'll not be so foolish again, I promise you.''

And if there was a ring in Lydia Derwent's words that sounded like prison doors closing, it was, so Pommy thought, no less than the truth.

6

Frederick Watters was not prompt. While his mother had promised that he would come before noon, he did not in fact arrive in Hanover Square until late afternoon.

Frederick was a man of medium height and undistinguished figure. His coat was by Weston, his boots by Hoby, but he wore them as though they had been carefully constructed for someone else. As for his features, Lady Playre had thought them so ordinary, she would not recognize him if she met him the next day.

Frederick found it hard to believe he was about to take a bride. He had not heretofore considered marriage save as an inconvenience affecting other people.

While it was true that he now wished to marry Pommy, and that he did not care a fig for any scandal that surrounded her, the cause of his generosity was not an overwhelming passion for his intended bride.

Scandal meant nothing to him, for he had not the slightest belief that Pommy had been compromised. She was not prone to look upon the opposite sex with any interest, and he did not move in elevated circles where manners and decorum were the rule. He was much more at home at Jackson's Gym or following the racing circuit than in any drawing room.

Her appeal to him lay solely in the only quality able to arouse admiration in him: her fortune was excessively large. Even her father's expeditions, which he had heard were enormously expensive, could not wipe it out.

If he did not rule her from the first, he knew without a doubt that she would cause him trouble. This very afternoon was no exception.

He presented himself at the house in Hanover Square, to be met in the foyer by Lady Playre. She glanced through the open front door and immediately voiced her objections.

"Mr. Watters, surely you are not driving Miss Fiske home in a closed carriage."

"My mother sent me," he said. "I didn't think it quite the thing myself, but she said that since we are betrothed and my only stop will be in Berkeley Square, it would make no difference. No one will know."

"I know your mother suggested the engagement would be announced, but I do not scruple to tell you that I consider it very shabby that you do this without Pommy's consent."

"The marriage," Frederick said indifferently, "has been arranged. Pommy will have to come around in time. Matter of fact, if I drove my phaeton, I couldn't be sure she might not give me the slip. No, ma'am, a carriage is safer."

Lady Playre was a victim of second thoughts. She had learned in one interview to despise Lady Derwent, and even her originally low opinion of Frederick was fast sinking even lower. She regretted that she had spent much of the previous day convincing Pommy that the best and indeed only responsible course for her was to return to her temporary guardian, and to trust Caroline to concoct a suitable plan to remove her from Lady Derwent's.

Caroline's intention, to which Gervase voiced no objection simply because he was not informed of it, was to write to her godmother, pleading Pommy's cause, and even, if necessary, go to Edgecumbe Manor herself. Caroline would be visiting at Lisle Court in a fortnight, for Justin's betrothal party—unless she could think of some ploy to blight Anilee's pretensions—and it was only a short drive from her childhood home to the dowager's.

However, Pommy Fiske, drawing on experience, had come to place no reliance on any plans made by others, especially those new to her acquaintance. Lady Playre was pleased to believe that her arguments had been cogent enough to persuade Pommy to docility, since the younger woman had become quiet, even compliant. Such demeanor, however, would have sounded alarm bells for those back at Beechknoll who knew her best.

Pommy ascended into the carriage, clutching all her belongings, not in a shawl this time but in a small valise borrowed from Lady Playre. Her mood was dark. She knew she must bide her time before making another bid for freedom. She would be watched closely, for a while, and it was necessary to give an impression of resignation for the immediate future.

Frederick disliked long silences. His proximity to Pommy in a closed carriage seemed an ideal opportunity for instructing his bride. As soon as the vehicle started to move, he began.

"I am pleased that you are no longer persisting in your headstrong ways. I know you realize how fortunate you are that your really outrageous behavior will not be the cause of ruin for you. I am willing to overlook your heavy-cavey performance in getting in some way out of my mother's house and over to Hanover Square. I wonder if you have any idea of how dangerous such a journey can be? You are indeed fortunate that no ruffian came upon you."

Not a ruffian, she thought, only a meddling, maddening man whose quick thinking had saved her from the watch.

But she would have been in no danger from the watch had he left her alone. The recollection of the watch, of course, brought her face to face with a thought she had kept purposely at bay these last hours.

He had indeed sheltered her from the watch. But his kiss still lingered on her lips. She had never been kissed before, at least seriously, and she had no idea that a man's arms around her, his lips on hers, could cause such a turmoil. Even now, remembering, she could feel the same throbbing warmth spreading down through her limbs, weakening her knees, and who knew what else might have happened had she not pulled away?

Even now, in the darkness of the coach, hearing but not listening to Frederick's monotonous voice, she felt her cheeks burn and her breath grow short.

She had pulled away, but not as promptly as a young lady should. In truth, a well-brought-up young lady would not have been standing in the street in the middle of the night, wrapped in a gentleman's evening cloak. Moreover, she was not at all sure she would resist next time . . . But there could be no next time.

Frederick droned on. "My mother thinks that we should be wed at once, before word of this disgrace gets out. Your reputation cannot stand much more damage, you know."

"My reputation? If it is so ruined, I wonder that your mother does not send me back to Beechknoll and wash her hands of me. If my reputation has been damaged beyond repair because I let my horse gallop in Hyde Park, or walked down Berkeley Street to Green Park without so much as an abigail with me, I must assume your mother knows best about London ways. But my character is without stain, Frederick, and you will know it."

"But you cannot get from Berkeley Square to Hanover Square alone. I do not accept that you were not abducted."

"I was not abducted, Frederick. I never thought your understanding was very sound, and now I am convinced of it. Pay attention to me, Frederick. I was not abducted. I was not seduced by anyone. I have not been harmed in the least. Your mother chooses to think I am not serious when I tell her I shall not marry you. Best believe me, Frederick, for I was never more in earnest."

Frederick said in a cheerful voice, "I have been told, you know, that ladies like to pretend shyness. But do not worry, Pommy, I shall not be put off by that."

She sighed heavily. She could, she knew, look forward to fifty years of this same kind of criticism—of her every move, which must be measured against some kind of standard to which she did not subscribe, criticism of her ideas, a calm certainty on his part that women were naught to the purpose, being of inferior wits.

Not fifty years, she amended, for she would kill herself first—or more likely, take a heavy instrument to him.

They must be approaching Berkeley Square. She was aware that the coach was slowing, probably to make the turn into the square. She looked from the window.

Frederick was again shocked. "Keep back! Don't show your face. You haven't the sense of a peahen. You want all the world to see you with me in a coach?"

Irritated, Pommy replied, "Surely it cannot be considered improper to ride in my guardian's coach? Where should I be safer?" A certain mocking note in her voice nettled him. He had no chance to reply, though, for she exclaimed sharply, "There's something amiss in the street."

There was indeed, although she never did discover what it was. There were shouts, dogs barking in different keys, and an assembly of persons gravitating toward the intersection. She recognized that they had traveled only as far as Conduit Street and were about to cross Bond Street,

a well-populated area. It was only moments before the coach
was surrounded by spectators, crowding forward to look at
something ahead of the coach.

Frederick, impatient and irritable, opened the door on his
side and called crossly to the coachman. "Get these people
out of the way. What's stopping us?"

Pommy did not wait to hear the details of this fortunate
incident. Quick as lightning, she grasped her borrowed valise
in one hand and opened the door next to her. Before
Frederick realized her intention, she had vanished in the
crowd.

At length, Frederick arrived, alone and more than usually
disheveled, at his mother's house.

"Gone? Frederick, I did not think even you could be such
a fool. Where did she go?"

"How do I know?" Frederick retorted, hard-pressed.
"She was out of sight before I knew she was out of the coach.
I looked everywhere, and what names some of those fools
in the street called me, I don't want to remember." He closed
his eyes and shuddered. "I don't think I want to marry such
a scapegrace as she is. Can't even shut her up in a coach
and have her stay where you put her. I'd never know what
fool thing she would do next."

"I know she does not want to marry you," his mother
said at last. "But I tell you frankly, I do not wish to see any
more of your creditors at my door."

"At your door? Here?" Frederick echoed, his eyes
anxious. "What did you tell them?"

"You must realize, Frederick, that I do not wish to have
anything to do with persons of that class. Creditors! They
were scruffy and vulgar, and I do not know what I should
say if someone of my acquaintance drove past and noticed

them standing on the steps. My steps. They said they could not find you."

"I haven't been to—to anywhere they could find me." He asked again, urgently, "What did you tell them?"

"What could I tell them? I told them I had no knowledge of your debts, nor would I pay them."

"My God," Frederick moaned. "They'll kill me."

His mother eyed him speculatively and without affection. She had not cared for her first husband, and Frederick resembled him all too closely. Like his father, her son would make a mull of everything he attempted.

"Kill you, Frederick? I hope you are not serious. But I did tell them," she added, relenting, "that you were about to make a very advantageous match, and they said they would consider that to your benefit. Now, of course, you've lost the bride."

Frederick could not find speech. since neither he nor Lady Derwent had been informed of Pommy's plan to travel—by stagecoach!—to Middlesex, the possibility that the girl might leave London did not occur to them.

"Well, we know where she will go," Lady Derwent said comfortably. "Back to Lady Playre's."

"You think so?"

She said simply, "Where else? She knows no one else in London. You can go tomorrow and inquire. It will do the girl good to worry overnight as to whether we will take her back or not. But, Frederick, I warn you. Do not let her escape again! I do not have the funds to pay your debts."

The next morning, Lady Playre received a second visit from Frederick Watters. Her conscience had troubled her in the night, and over her breakfast chocolate she considered various schemes that might appease the inner voice that told her she had unequivocally thrown Pommy to the wolves.

She had finally made up her mind that she would pay a call on Lady Derwent and indicate as strongly as civility allowed that Pommy had friends with influence and credit in the world. A warning, that was all, but nonetheless sincere.

Blaise's announcement of the arrival of Mr. Watters alarmed her. Had something already happened to Pommy? How could it? She had been gone only overnight.

Something indeed had. When Frederick had unburdened himself, Lady Playre rose from her chair in agitation. "Pommy gone! You wish to marry her and you cannot even convey her safely to Berkeley Square?" she railed. "But if she escaped yesterday afternoon, she could be anywhere by now. What have you done to find her? Where have you looked? Where could she have spent the night?"

At that moment Justin sauntered through the open salon door. Blaise stood behind him ready to relieve him of his driving coat, but Justin, surprised at the scene before him, made no move to remove even his gloves.

"Caroline, what is amiss? That flush on your cheeks—"
Speechless, she merely gestured toward Frederick.

"I don't see that it is any of your affair, Lord Rutledge," Frederick said sullenly. "But the truth of the matter is that Miss Fiske has run away. Again."

"When?" demanded Justin. "This morning?"

Caroline found her voice. "Last night. On the way home from here. And they think she came here." A thought struck her. Had the girl gone to Justin himself?

Her brother answered the question in her eyes. "No. Not here either? Then," he said coolly, turning to Frederick, "we shall hope for your sake that no harm has come to her. Overnight in London, a delicately nurtured young lady—"

"A hobbledehoy," muttered Frederick.

"And if she has not been robbed of everything and is now floating in the river—"

"Dear God, no!" Caroline cried.

"—you may count yourself fortunate, Mr. Watters. You and that mother of yours have driven her to take such extreme measures, and you may believe me when I say I shall see that you pay for any damage, however slight, Miss Fiske has sustained."

Justin's icy voice, even more than his stern words, caused great uneasiness in the region of Frederick's stomach, and an unbecoming flush crept up his cheeks. Justin did not notice. Indeed, he stood like a man struck by a clear but startling idea.

"I—I'll get her back," Frederick said hastily. "I'll set the Bow Street Runners after her. She won't have gone far."

Justin returned to himself with a start. "Runners?" he said, his voice dripping with contempt. "Your privilege, of course. But think of your friends. They will say, since your betrothal has just been made public, that your bride will go to any lengths rather than wed you, and you set the runners on her like a common criminal."

Slowly, Frederick said, "I hadn't thought of that."

"Think of it, then," Justin said inexorably. "She was in your carriage, I believe you said? And what vulgar advances did you make that caused her to flee?"

Caroline said, "I did not approve of the closed carriage."

Frederick was moved to ill-advised anger. Lord Rutledge he knew only by reputation, since the two moved in entirely different circles. But a gentleman can take only so many insults before honor must be defended.

"I merely spoke to her. I certainly did nothing—"

Caroline interposed, "That is the shame of it, Mr. Watters. She has been gone since yesterday afternoon, and only now you begin to search for her? Abominable!"

"But he cannot insult me. I demand an apology."

Too late Frederick realized that he was challenging one

of the finest pistol shots in England. Moreover, that dangerous man was at the moment seething with anger directed, however unjust Frederick might deem it, at him.

"I will meet you," Justin told him, "at any time you wish. But in the meantime, I beg you will leave my sister's house." Frederick reached the door, held wide open by Blaise. Justin added, "I do recommend that you go somewhere and contemplate your sins. Particularly those in connection with Miss Fiske."

The door closed behind his sister's caller before Justin spoke. "Caroline, my dear," he said in a warm voice, "pray do not weep. The girl will most likely come to no harm before I fetch her back."

"Fetch her back?" She looked at him with amazement, tears running down her cheeks. "Justin, I have grown so fond of Pommy. I know I've known her only a matter of hours, but she has such a sweet disposition."

Sweetness was what Justin remembered too—a beguiling sweetness, and he was not mistaken, she did respond to his kiss, her arms stealing up around his neck as he held her safe and trembling under his cloak.

But it would be disastrous to allow his thoughts to stray in that direction. "Don't fret," he said with a return to his usual brisk manner. "I'll find her."

"Where could she be? I do wish she had come back here to me. But she knows so few people in London."

Justin laughed briefly. He was beginning to understand Pommy. "If she is not on the stage to Middlesex at this moment, I'll commit myself to Bedlam."

7

Soon after dawn, the morning after Pommy's informal departure from Frederick and his mother's coach, the yard of the Swan with Two Necks, in Lad Lane just off Gresham Street, was full of activity.

The day coaches were pulled out of the stables into the yard, their horses, ostlers at their heads, backed between the shafts, and harness buckled into place. On the far side of the yard the overnight coaches were pulling wearily in. Their human freight and the horses alike seemed to be in the last stages of fatigue, and a few of the passengers on alighting were forced to cling to the coach doors until they worked the painful cramp out of their legs.

The coffee room was furnishing gallons of tea and coffee, pigeon pie, boiled beef, and hot muffins to incoming travelers, ravenous now the perils of the night journey lay behind them.

However, the poor day passengers had only time for a bracing nip of brandy and water before they were bundled into their stagecoaches. Pommy declined to start a long day fortified only by brandy. For one thing, she was not sure the motion of the coach would not make her sick, and for another, she was quite stimulated enough at the moment.

She counted the coins left, after she had paid for a night's lodging in a room off the second gallery, which she shared with three other females. The weight of her coins, she decided ruefully, would not greatly discommode her, for there were only two left.

Pommy was a prudent person, at least sometimes, and she stifled her pangs of hunger in favor of having a little money in case her grandmother refused to welcome her. Just in case, she thought . . . But her spirits slipped even lower than before.

She moved restlessly toward the coaches being readied for the road. She was terrified lest she miss her proper coach and would need to stay another night at the Swan. A day's delay in leaving London could well give Frederick time to remember her maternal grandmother. He probably would not come after her, since his affections were not engaged, but then again, he might.

Pommy had no illusions as to the quality of Frederick's wish to marry her. She knew it was only for her fortune. How strange to think that her wealth was the cause of her present circumstance, and yet she had not enough money to buy a proper breakfast.

At length she found the proper vehicle, was assured several times that this coach truly was going to Bristol along the Bath Road, and was helped up the steps. She was the first passenger to board. She sat in the corner of the forward-facing seat and gave herself up to gloomy thoughts. It was of no use to conjecture what the day might bring, so her mind strayed to the day before.

While she was still in Lady Playre's house, she had garnered certain information that was now proving useful. How fortunate it was that Lady Playre had grown up next to Pommy's grandmother's retirement cottage. Such a co-incidence should be considered providential.

Pommy knew her grandmother's home was near Hammondsworth, and her initial plan had been simply to travel to that town and then inquire her way from there. But Lady Playre had, quite innocently, revealed that the way was shorter to leave the coach at Harlington. Since her remarks, primarily centering on Lisle Court, her brother's estate, could easily be adapted to refer to the dowager duchess's home, Edgecumbe Manor, Pommy tucked information away for future use like a squirrel spurred by the first winds of autumn.

The occasion for future use arose immediately. Later that same day, as it happened. Pommy had not believed that a second opportunity would be hers so soon. When Frederick's coach was stopped by some trouble in the street, Pommy did not need to think twice. She was out of the coach and lost in the crowd in a minute.

The hours after that, however, were less pleasant. She was thankful for her unfashionable country cloak, for she blended into the jostling crowds. She was accosted more than once, but she evaded them all. She had to ask directions again and again, but at last she arrived at her destination. She bought her supper and her night's lodging at the Swan with Two Necks, and there was nothing more to do until she reached Harlington.

With a start she realized that the coach was moving. Other travelers had filled the coach and now there was a full complement of passengers inside.

They were barely under way before she realized that riding in a public stage was not in the least like traveling in her father's coach. For a moment, she felt sorry for herself. The only people who really wanted her were those she could not abide, and they wanted her for the wrong reasons. And what she would do if Grandmother turned her out, as seemed probable, she did not know.

She only recently came to know her grandmother's name.

Her father had not allowed that name to be spoken at Beech-knoll, but he could not control every tongue. Pommy's last governess had a very rigid view of what was proper, and "family" was at the forefront of the subjects Miss Horne deemed vital for a young lady to know.

It was not proper to ignore one's grandmother, so Miss Horne believed, so Pommy was informed that her mother's family name was Sundon, that her grandmother was Lady Eleanor Edgecumbe Sundon, was the dowager Duchess of Woodburn.

"But, Miss Horne, if she is the dowager, then who is the duke? My uncle?"

"No, my dear, your mother, Julia, was the only child. I have been told that the title and lands went to some distant branch of the family."

Just recently, Lady Derwent had, so she claimed to Lady Playre, written to the duchess about Pommy and received word that the girl would not be welcome. But Pommy knew that her Cousin Lydia was not truthful at times, and she prayed that this was one such occasion.

But sufficient unto the day was the evil thereof, decided Pommy, and turned her attention to her fellow passengers. The woman opposite her was clearly a farmer's wife, round and cheerful and apple-cheeked—appropriate, Pommy thought, since she was carrying on her lap a small basket of apples as rosy-hued as the woman herself.

Next to her sat a thin woman past her first youth, with a long face and a pinched look about her, as though she had not eaten well for months. This morning Pommy could sympathize with her. She seemed to be in charge of the weedy young man beside her, dressed in black and wearing a clerical collar.

The two passengers beside Pommy on the seat facing forward were a mother and daughter, traveling, if one could believe what the older woman said, on a level below their quality. "My husband," the mother told them earnestly, "does not know we are returning from London a week early, or he would have sent our own coach for us. And when he finds we rode on the public stage, I do not know what he will say."

The daughter, perhaps fourteen, rolled her eyes in a most unfilial manner, but said nothing.

After the other passengers had exchanged what personal information they wished, the farmer's wife turned to Pommy. "Just call me Mrs. Appersett," she said. "And where might you be bound, dearie?"

Pommy, thus addressed, was startled. She had not expected to be a part of the social life evolving within the coach, but she was incapable of snubbing the woman. And, for all Pommy really knew, she might well be joining the working class before the end of the week.

"I'm going to visit my grandmother," she said softly, afraid her voice would falter. It did not.

"Ah," responded the bright-eyed Mrs. Appersett. "Your granny'll be glad to see you, to be sure."

A little hysterically, Pommy wondered what her companions would say were she to inform them that Granny was the dowager Duchess of Woodburn. Probably gape with disbelief and turn her over to the nearest magistrate with a strong recommendation to put her in Bedlam.

The thin woman approved of Pommy. She did not think that the girl was attractive enough to woo her brother from his religious calling, being far too thin. That unfortunate scrape the young curate had recently fallen into, and been removed from with great difficulty and a promise of eternal vigilance on the part of his family, had nearly been the end of his career in the Church. But that woman was fat as a barrel.

The curate's sister was willing enough to pass the time in conversation.

"Family is so important," she informed them. "My brother Horace is going to a new cure, quite distant, beyond Bristol, in fact, and I cannot see him go alone, you know. It will make a great deal of difference to Horace to have a member of his family to keep house for him."

A spectator might have been pardoned for thinking that the new curate's opinion had not been invited. Pommy saw his mouth tighten and a curious hunted look appear in his eyes. He turned his attention to the landscape passing by.

The fourteen-year-old, whose name, it developed, was Florence, was a bright young lady. The hood of Pommy's cloak had fallen back, and Florence gazed at Pommy with admiration. She leaned forward and spoke past her mother. "Those curls—how do you get them to fall forward like that?"

Her mother said futilely, "Now, Florence."

Pommy froze for a moment. She had taken thought to her dress and to her manner, but she had not been careful enough. Her hair was dressed, not in the newest fashion, but definitely not plainly. Lady Derwent's maid had a rare talent with her comb and brushes.

"It is naturally like this," Pommy said, adding with truth, "I have very little to do with it."

Mrs. Appersett with a pointed stare at Pommy's hands nodded. "It's plain you were a lady's maid, dearie. Those soft hands never did no kitchen work. I heard that lady's maids can call their own tune as far as money goes?"

"A fribble of a job," the curate's sister said. "I approve your giving it up."

"But I—" began Pommy, and then decided there was little use in protesting. No matter what her companions concluded, they could not come close to the truth. And she would be leaving the coach soon, anyway.

Mrs. Appersett was one who as soon as any vehicle in which she rode started—be it stagecoach or farm cart—became ravenously hungry. Now she offered her basket of apples to the passengers, and Pommy took one with gratitude. She would be hard-pressed, she thought, not to fall on it like a starving animal. When she had eaten half, reveling in the juicy sweetness descending to her stomach, she realized that her situation, being considered somewhat out of the ordinary, was still under discussion by her companions.

"I've heard about the goings-on by the quality," Mrs. Appersett said sagely. "How the young gentlemen of the house think the maids is put there for their pleasure. Is it so?"

"I really cannot say," said Pommy, mouth full. She recalled suddenly the behavior of Lord Rutledge, who had thought she was a maidservant. Shameful, she thought, and reddened, with shame or remembered pleasure, she could not have said.

"A 'course you can't," said Mrs. Appersett, "but I reckon you've answered right enough. That pink on your cheeks is worth a hundred words, to be sure. I'd be surprised to hear that you aren't on the run because of just that kind of scandal."

"A maid's reputation is her only wealth," pronounced the curate. "Very wise to preserve it."

"I keep a very close watch on my maids," Florence's mother said.

Florence said in a low voice that only Pommy heard, "All one of them."

The coach trundled on its way, the passengers it carried being well-pleased with one another's company.

Without encouragement from Pommy, the others decided

that she had been the object of advances from her employer's dastardly son, although Florence and her mother held out for the husband, and in spite of all her maidenly protests, she had been forced to flee in the night to preserve her reputation.

"Carrying naught but that little handbag," Mrs. Appersett pointed out. "Stands to reason she didn't have time to pack."

She, they concluded, was returning to Granny for shelter, and it was hoped, again by Mrs. Appersett, that Granny would not be put off by the la-di-da London ways she had obviously picked up in her employment.

Pommy lost interest in their conversation and began to wonder how far it was to Harlington. She leaned forward to look from the window. It was at that moment that the smart curricle, the matched bays driven expertly and fast by a top-of-the-trees gentleman, passed the coach.

"The fool," said the curate. "Endangering everybody on the road."

Mrs. Appersett nodded. "Right enough! But my, those horses are handsome ones. Not to pull a wagon, mind you."

Florence's eyes shone with admiration. "Handsome," she breathed, and it was clear that she did not refer to the cattle.

Predictably, her mother said, "Now, Florence. Handsome is as handsome does."

And Pommy, recognizing the driver as he passed, near enough for her to touch had they been standing still, said, "Oh, I am undone."

Florence, craning to watch the driver as far as she could, suddenly exclaimed, "What's he doing that for? He's stopping."

"Well," her mother said sourly, "don't gawk at him. Not likely he's stopped for you, my girl."

Mrs. Appersett was as shrewd as the horse-copers her husband dealt with. She fixed her eyes on Pommy and found confirmation of her suspicions in the girl's ashen face and apprehensive eyes.

"Lass, he's the villain chasing after you, ain't he? He's no schoolboy. Your mistress's husband, not a doubt. Well, we'll just see about him."

Lord Rutledge was proven right in his judgment, he thought as he overtook the Bath coach. The girl must be on it, and while he told himself he did not care what happened to a fool of a girl who would not listen to reason and who turned out to be so unbiddable there was no dealing with her, yet he had left London some time since with the object of finding her and delivering her safely to somebody.

That idiot Watters could not even carry the girl across London in a carriage without losing her. Well, Justin Harcourt, Lord Rutledge, came of different stock. There had been Crusaders in his family, lords who had served their king on the Field of the Cloth of Gold, in India and in Europe, and none of them lacked courage.

It took only, thought Justin, a precise goal and a firm stand, and these were exactly the virtues that Watters lacked. But the duchess's granddaughter was quite above Watters' touch, and it seemed to Justin that, having taken a hand in the girl's romantic escapade, he had an obligation. Not to her, but to himself. He must set Miss Fiske back on her feet again and then he could dismiss her from his mind.

He wished he could be sure she had got away from London safely and not been murdered on the streets or robbed on Hampstead Heath and left under a bush.

Now he had overtaken the coach, and he had from the corner of his eye caught a glimpse of a female within who he thought could be Pommy. However, the windows of the coach were filmed with dirt and he could not be sure.

Taking his usual direct course to what he wanted, he swung

his vehicle across the road and waited for the coach to come to a lumbering halt.

The coachman's opinions of this arrogant action on the part of the dandy, sitting calm as you please in his curricle, were expressed vocally with some heat. Fortunately his words were not audible to the six inside passengers.

Brakes squealed, the coach stood nearly on its nose, the six passengers were all tumbled about, and with a sound like a shot the window curtain fell.

"Lord a'mighty, it's a highwayman. We'll all be robbed and worse," Florence's mother cried. She continued to cry out, even though the others begged her to be quiet so they could hear the conversation ahead. Only Florence's firm hand across her mother's mouth proved effective.

Pommy listened, appalled. The strong resonant voice of Lord Rutledge demanded, "How many passengers do you carry?"

"Six."

"You'll be traveling on with five," Justin informed him. "One of them is a runaway, and I'll take her."

"Take her where?" said the coachman, suspicious. "You don't look like a runner to me."

"We come in all shapes and sizes," Justin improvised. "Now, I'll just take a look at your fares."

"Good thing for him this isn't the mail," murmured the curate. "He'd been shot."

"Hsst," said the farmer's wife. "Runaway?" she whispered hoarsely to Pommy. "Does he mean you?"

"I'm afraid so," Pommy answered miserably, seeing captivity again ahead of her.

If Pommy had ever considered herself to be impulsive in running away, prompt to improvise when opportunity offered—such as a tumult in the street only yesterday—she was now to see an expert at work.

"Down," said Mrs. Appersett to Pommy, rather as though to an untrained dog. "Down on the floor."

At the same moment, she handed her basket of apples unceremoniously to the curate's sister and commandeered that lady's lap rug. Dissatisfied with Pommy's lack of response, she pulled her down to her knees on the floor.

Belatedly catching the enthusiasm of the moment, Pommy crouched on the floor of the coach. While all of William Chaplin's coaches were cleaned at the Swan with Two Necks before they took the road, yet Pommy's first breath in her new position was redolent of straw and dust. She put her finger under her nose in a childish attempt to stifle a sneeze. For the moment, the remedy worked.

There was no time to waste. The conversation at the horses' heads had ceased, and the approaching steps of booted feet could be heard.

"Quick," urged the farmer's wife again. Her whispered orders came to Pommy's ears muffled by the lap rug.

Florence helped Mrs. Appersett spread the lap rug over the figure huddled on the floor so that Pommy appeared to be merely a misshapen bundle of indeterminate content— perhaps old clothes.

Pommy, enveloped by the lap rug, the formidable smell of camphor added to the previous mixture, gave up the uneven struggle and sneezed. It was a small sound and did not carry. But her control was sorely tried when she felt the basket of apples set on the middle of her back, followed by Mrs. Appersett's feet on her shoulders, next to the door.

The door, only inches from Pommy's head, opened abruptly, and she was aware of the rustle of unexplained movement around her.

She would have enjoyed seeing Lord Rutledge's expression at that moment. He was certain that Pommy would be on the coach seeking refuge in her grandmother's home. He had not mentioned to his sister all of the reasons that had driven him hastily out of London to retrieve Pommy from her headlong flight.

First, of course, was that Miss Fiske was no wiser in the ways of the world than a newly weaned kitten. Since he had interfered at the start, it seemed incumbent upon him to see her safely into the hands of someone who cared about her. From the little he had learned of Pommy's relatives, no one of that caliber leapt immediately to the mind.

It seemed to him that the dowager duchess was no better than Lady Derwent on that head. While he did not believe truth was always on Lady Derwent's tongue, yet her statement that the duchess had refused to receive her grand-daughter might be true. And if it were, someone needed to be at hand for the girl. It did not occur to him to wonder why he took on this chore so readily.

Now, having overtaken the coach and stopped it, all that remained was to pluck Pommy off the vehicle and take her the twenty miles from this spot to Edgecumbe Manor. The sun was still high, and they could make the journey in full daylight.

He stood at the open stagecoach door and said, "Pommy!"

No answer came. He looked in turn at a large red-cheeked woman, a thin man wearing a clerical collar, two other women, and a fresh-faced girl who leaned forward and fixed him with a frankly idolizing stare. But no Pommy.

The passengers were not taking his interruption of their journey lightly.

"Paid for my passage, I did, and the company said naught about getting stopped every whip stitch," said Mrs. Appersett, adopting a belligerent tone.

"I must say you look like a gentleman," said the curate, losing his shyness in the common cause. "What misfortunes you must have seen to bring you as low as to be robbing honest folk on the stage.''

They seemed, thought Justin, to be the most restless group of people he had ever seen. They moved. It was difficult to distinguish one from another. The only one of the passengers who did not seem to be afflicted with Saint Vitus' dance was the young girl. Her fixed look of pure adoration unnerved him, as it was intended to do.

''Pommy?'' he inquired. Addressing the farmer's wife, who seemed to have an addiction to apples, judging from the full basket she steadied on the shapeless luggage under her feet, he asked, ''Wasn't there a young person on the stage when you left London? I know there was. Where did she leave the coach?''

Mrs. Appersett said, ''Bless you, my lord, for I can see there's naught of the Bow Street Runner about you. And why else would you be pursuing a poor girl? We've all been together since we started. No one got off—we'd 'a seen. A young woman? There's just those of us now in the coach that started out.''

He suspected . . . he did not know what. But the bright-blue eyes of the large woman seemed cheerfully innocent. He glanced at the other passengers. No answers there.

With a stifled oath, he slammed the door. The bundle stirred under Mrs. Appersett's feet, and she said, ''Not yet, dearie. Wait till he's long gone.'' Nevertheless, as a sign that danger receded, she removed her feet from Pommy's shoulders.

When they were once again under way, the passengers gave way to unbridled glee. Even Florence's mother said, ''And nobody had to lie.''

''I should have had to deplore,'' said the curate, ''bearing false witness. However—''

"But we told the truth. Tell the truth and shame the devil, I always say. And we did," crowed Mrs. Appersett. "I just said, everyone in the coach—"

"And if we moved around," the curate's sister said, with a titter, "so that he could not count us—if he thought there were six of us rather than five, I am sure we are not to blame for his mistake."

She was interrupted by a convulsion apparently in the lap rug. The apple basket tipped over and the part of the rug next to the door stood upright as Pommy at last gave vent to the prodigious sneeze that had been gathering force for some minutes.

"Oh, my," said the curate's sister, guiltily aware that the excitement of the plot had quite overshadowed the welfare of the victim.

Once restored to her seat and provided with an apple from the basket, Pommy thanked them all.

"You were so clever," she told them, "and you certainly saved me." She continued in the same vein for some time as she kept watch in vain for a curricle on the road ahead.

She had not thought he would given up so easily. Certainly he had been persistent enough in preventing her escape at the start of her flight.

As the miles unrolled beneath the wheels, she felt her spirits sinking lower and lower. She had escaped from Cousin Lydia and Frederick, all well and good.

But did she want to escape from Lord Rutledge?

8

Justin's splendid bays were swiftly putting distance between the curricle and the stagecoach, progressing heavily behind on the road to Bath. He paid little heed to his driving. Instead, he turned over in his mind the recent events that led to his present confusion.

At the door of the coach Justin had been as baffled as though he had driven into a brick wall that had not been in place yesterday. He felt that although his acquaintance with Pommy was of short duration, it made up in intensity what it lacked in time, and he believed he knew how she would go on.

He knew Caroline had planned to write on Pommy's behalf to the duchess, and had made no objection. But Pommy had clearly learned to place no trust in orderly procedures and well-planned schemes. She seized the first opportunity to give that nincompoop Frederick the slip, and Justin would have wagered a fortune on Pommy's being on that coach.

Could she have taken an earlier coach? No. This was the first of the day. And she would not have lingered in London for a later one. Unless, of course, she had been waylaid, robbed, and worse, and now was bound and gagged in a noisome Cheapside cellar.

If she were not on that coach, then, where was she?

However, at this moment he was more angry than worried. Unreasonably, he blamed Pommy for the *contretemps* just past. He would not soon forget that he had just now been made a fool of. Those bucolic faces had stared unwinking at him, disapproving of him, telling him he was on a fool's errand, that no such person had ever been on the stage.

Indeed, they had, he decided, looked at him as though he were a villain of noble lineage in dastardly pursuit of an innocent country maid. A farce fit only for a stage at a country fair! Revolted by the idea, he set his bays on at an increased pace. There was nothing more he could do about the abominable Miss Fiske at the moment. Indeed, he could almost find a pity in his heart for Frederick Watters—or whomever she might marry.

Casting his thoughts ahead, he found pleasure in considering that in less than four hours he would be driving through the great and ancient gates of Lisle Court. Even though his servants did not expect him for a sennight, he was assured of generous fires, a well-aired bed, and a hot dinner exquisitely prepared by Pierre, his expensive French chef.

Since Justin's greatest contentment was found at his country estates, he made sure as well of his comforts there. His thoughts, naturally enough, turned then to his approaching marriage.

He entertained strong reservations about his union with Miss Mortimer. He suspected, having become acquainted with his affianced bride, that there was nothing about which they might agree. She certainly would not choose to ride out with him over his acres. Nor was she possessed of more than a rudimentary education, and while he did not expect to wed a classical scholar, he did wish that Anilee had at the very least a nodding acquaintance with the likes of William Shakespeare.

Finding his reflections on that head to be unprofitable, he allowed his thoughts to drift back to Miss Fiske. He had never felt such a fool, and he had Miss Fiske to thank. She should have been on that coach.

His memory showed him the undistinguished and doltish faces filling the stagecoach. Something tugged at his mind then, something that had left him puzzled at the time and still was unclear. Unconsciously he slowed his bays and thought hard.

Painstakingly, he reviewed the entire episode: the coachman, saying there were six passengers; the passengers themselves, "No one left the coach."

If they started with six, it was to be assumed they were six when he stopped them.

Of course he had seen all six! Hadn't he?

There was the large woman, the staring child, the clergyman and the woman with him, the staring child's mother. That was only five. But there had been no room for more.

His bays were moving now at a walking pace while he concentrated. He began again to count. The large woman with the apples . . . with the apples! That was it. Something about the basket of apples, the woman's feet in country boots next to them, supported by rug-covered baggage of some kind . . .

There were six passengers in the coach. And where was the sixth? Under the apple basket. There could be no doubt of it.

Whether that sixth passenger was Miss Melpomene Fiske or not was the only doubt left. But who else would think she had reason to disguise herself with an apple basket?

With a string of oaths he did not bother to stifle, he backed his curricle around and started back the way he had come.

The stagecoach, trying to make up the time lost by the un-

official and indeed illegal halt forced by the top-lofty
gentleman in search of a runaway, traveled fast. The next
scheduled stop at Osterley would be time enough for refresh-
ment for passengers and stage men alike, and after some time
they pulled up at the White Horse.

The White Horse, one of many of similar name in England, stood on the far side of the town as they came in from
the direction of London. It was a low timbered building, next
to an unwalled yard in which no vehicles could be seen.

The five friendly passengers departed the coach as one,
appetites stimulated by the drama they had just staged.
Pommy, all too conscious of the meager contents of her
purse, did not move.

"I'm not hungry," she lied to Mrs. Appersett in response
to her bracing invitation to "light and eat."

"Too much excitement." The curate's sister nodded
sagely. "I know when my brother was ordained, I couldn't
take more than a cup of tea for a week." And during her
brother's "trouble" she had lost two stone, she remembered.

Before she started toward the inn, Mrs. Appersett pressed
another apple into Pommy's hands. However, it was Florence
who understood. "Here's a cake I've had by me in case we
didn't stop anywhere. No, no, take it. I'm getting too fat
anyway." In a lower voice she added, "I'd lose my appetite,
too, if I let a prize like that slip out of my hands. If I was
you, I'd think twice and then again."

"Now, Florence," Pommy said, in unconscious imitation
of the girl's mother. She ate the cake, slowly savoring it.
When it was gone, she licked all the crumbs from her fingers.
One trouble with being independent, she decided, was that
you seemed to be hungry all the time.

There were still no signs of the passengers returning. Her
left leg began to cramp. She looked carefully around the yard
and saw no one. She opened the door and jumped to the

ground. Her knee buckled and she hung on to the door latch for a moment.

She needed to walk. Holding the valise that contained her jewel case close to her, she took a few tentative steps. At once she began to feel better, and she lengthened her stride. Used as she had been to riding over Beechknoll every day, the weeks in London, besides being made miserable by Lady Derwent's constant nagging, had curtailed her outdoor exercise.

How good it felt to step out smartly in the fresh air, redolent of familiar stable odors. It was almost like being home again.

She walked at first toward the inn and then turned to walk along the long side of the building. She had come so far from London, and her new friends had repelled her would-be captor. It could not be far to Edgecumbe Manor.

Intoxicated by her good fortune so far, she failed to hear the jingle of harness and a soft equine whuffle quite close at hand. She passed the end of the building and turned to retrace her steps.

A swift step behind her, a large and fortunately clean hand clapped over her mouth and a strong arm around her waist, sweeping her from off her feet. Before she could think what was happening to her, she was lifted to the curricle seat and Lord Rutledge was driving away with her.

She struggled in his grasp, but the arm around her waist tightened, leaving her not enough breath to scream.

"No use to scream," came Justin's voice in her ear as though in answer to her thought.

But while she could not escape, her mouth was free, and she proceeded to share her opinions with him. "Of course there is no need to scream. Who would hear if I did?"

"All the inhabitants of Osterley," he said calmly.

"And they wouldn't help me. Not like my friends in the coach."

"They might," Justin said, "but think of the scandal. Granddaughter of the Duchess of Woodburn, instigating riots and civil disobedience in the streets."

"Don't think you would escape censure," Pommy pointed out waspishly. "You kidnapped me."

Justin smiled. "But by the time you convinced everyone you are indeed her grace's daughter—even if you could persuade the rustics of that fact—I would be well out of it, you know."

He spoke only truth, and Pommy fell silent. Some little way farther along the road, he turned off onto a less-traveled route.

She spoke again, but only to say with dignity, "Pray remove your arm, sir. I shall not try to get away."

He removed his arm quickly. He had forgotten he still held her. Somehow it had felt so natural.

At length, she ventured, "Where are you taking me, sir?"

"To your grandmother. Where else?"

"I did not know."

He glanced at her. "Good God, girl, do you think I'm such a loose screw as to run off with you myself?"

"No, my lord."

"Call me Justin."

"But, you see, I do not know precisely where I am, and you must admit you forced me to go with you before . . . Was it only two nights since?"

"It was. And a fine mess you've made in two days."

He did not know why he lashed out at her so savagely, and the moment the words left his lips, he wished for them back again. It was not this slip of a green girl that caused his aversion to his forthcoming marriage and his resulting ill temper. That reluctance was of long standing. But in the last two days, reluctance had become active dislike.

But it was not Pommy's fault, and not quite handsomely, he told her so. "Whatever mess we're in, my dear, it is my fault as much as yours." When she did not answer, he looked closely at her. "You're crying, Miss Fiske. What did I say?"

"If you had just let me alone . . ."

With an air of great reasonableness, he pointed out, "But I did take you safely to my sister's."

"What has that to do with today?"

"So today I shall take you safely to your grandmother."

They drove for a couple of miles before Pommy, forgetting her resentment of his high-handed ways, said in a small voice, "Do you think she'll take me in?"

"Of course she will," said Justin staunchly, ignoring the fact that it was his own doubts on this very head that launched him in pursuit of her down the Bath Road.

They came to a small village. Justin drove down the high street without slackening his pace. It was doubtful if he even saw chickens, dogs, and some few people scattering out of the way of the bays.

Once beyond the last houses, he resumed. "There was a quarrel? I don't recall hearing about it. I suppose I was too young to be told."

"I don't know much about it myself. It happened before I was born. My governess Miss Horne told me, but she couldn't have been there."

"Probably made inquiries. No family has secrets that the servants don't know. How she came to know is not to the point. What did she tell you?"

"Just that Mama married my father because her mother forbade her to see him again. You know, I think my mother must have been too much indulged in her youth."

"You may be right. Of course, in that case her grace would have been better advised to let the affair run its course."

She glanced sharply at him. Did he mean, she wondered, that he might not marry Miss Anilee Mortimer after all if his sister dropped her opposition to the match?

She continued. "And after I was born and Mama died, my father threatened my grandmother that she would never see me again—ever—unless he got the emeralds. Truly," she said, turning to look at Justin, "I do not understand."

Justin knew they were only an hour's drive away from Edgecumbe Manor. The more he heard from Miss Fiske, the higher he judged the odds against her finding a happy home with the duchess.

"Probably a question of jewels as part of your mother's inheritance. But don't worry," he added kindly, "we'll know soon enough."

There were many unanswered questions in her mind as well. Justin was right: they would soon know. They . . . But she was not sure he would stay to beard the dragon with her. Perhaps he would make her alight at the gates—she supposed there would be gates at a duke's entrance—and she must then walk alone in the gathering twilight to the house.

If Papa had told the duchess she would never see her granddaughter again, then why would Cousin Lydia say her grace had refused to take her? She doubted that Papa had even considered sending her to the duchess. Would Lady Derwent lie that outrageously?

"What I do remember," Pommy said, not knowing she intended to speak until she heard her own voice, "is that someone came. It must have been my grandmother, who else? A lady who smelled so good. Her hands were soft, and she never came again. I longed for years for her to come back, but I never knew who she was."

Justin inquired, "Is that all you remember?"

Slowly searching the memory that had long been hidden

away, she said, "There was more. Loud voices, I think, and I remember a door slamming. And that's all."

"The famous quarrel, you think?"

"It's possible. I think I couldn't have been more than four years old."

They left the road they had traveled since leaving the Bath Road. Now they drove between dust-covered fences of hawthorn and other shrubs that Pommy did not recognize.

"We're nearly there," Justin assured her. In a gentler tone, he added, "Sorry you came?"

She confided, "I was always one for giving way to impulses I later regretted. Usually, all turns out well enough. No disasters, I mean, so far. But I confess I do not know quite what I will do if she turns me away. It does seem more and more likely to me that she really doesn't want me, even if she remembers after all this time that I exist."

"She wouldn't forget, even though she might ignore you."

"Cousin Lydia said—"

"Blast Cousin Lydia! If you believe a word that woman says, you're even more gullible than I think," Justin burst out savagely. "I cannot have any consideration for her after what she has done to you."

Pommy stared at him, surprised by the heat with which he spoke.

"Betrothing you to that Watters fool, in case you have forgotten. And Caroline said the woman was supposed to bring you into society? And refused?"

"She said," Pommy whispered, "that I was uncivilized. And she may be right, and my grandmother will be disgusted with me."

Justin placed his hand awkwardly on her arm in apology. "Forgive me. I know you are well aware of the damage done to you. I'm not angry with you."

In a moment, Pommy regained her poise. "At least the weather is fine."

He chuckled. "Did you think we'd become mired in the mud if it rained?"

"Oh no, I know you would not. But I should think the hedges would be most uncomfortable for sleeping if the weather turns foul."

"You wretched girl! You'll not sleep in hedgerows while I have anything to say to it."

"But you wouldn't," she said sagely. "I may not be up to the mark, as I have often been told, at least recently, but even I know it would be totally ineligible for you to take an interest in my situation."

Justin could have pointed out that he was enmeshed to the hilt already in an "ineligible" situation that gave no sign of resolving itself, but he said nothing. He was in truth unable to mark the precise steps that had led him to this present moment. When he had left his club two nights ago, he would have shouted with derision at the possibility of tooling down a country lane with a young lady of quality, without either an abigail or a groom and not a soul in the world knowing where they were.

"Sir—"

"Call me Justin," he repeated.

"Justin," she began again obediently, "perhaps I could find shelter in one of your barns?"

He burst into a laugh of unfeigned delight. Suddenly he realized that he had enjoyed these last few hours, angry as he had been at the start. His companion was sweet-natured, intelligent, and greatly to be admired for her courage and determination. He had even forgotten Anilee Mortimer. The headlong flight of time racing toward his marriage was halted for this little while with the lively and ingenuous Miss Fiske. There was significance, he suspected, in the realization that the absence of Anilee in his thoughts made room for a seldom-experienced happiness.

Dropping back into reality with an unwelcome thud, he busied himself with the need to consider alternatives for the courageous, uncomplaining young lady at his side. The duchess might well refuse to recognize her granddaughter. Justin knew the duchess, of course, but he had been away from England for some years. Even before he left, he was aware of her reputation for intrigue and intransigence. He wished heartily that Miss Fiske had waited long enough for Caroline to pave the way with the duchess by letter. If anyone could melt the duchess's heart—assuming it had frozen toward Pommy—it was Lady Playre. His sister and her reclusive godmother had much in common.

Justin considered it likely that the duchess bore a good share of the blame for the family rift, no matter what the stated cause. She was a lady of pronounced opinions and no reluctance to share them.

If she remained unforgiving, against all decency, Miss Fiske might well be searching for a convenient hedgerow by nightfall.

He might, as a temporary measure, settle her with one of his tenant families, but he could think of none whose members' tongues were not hinged in the middle. He would send at once for Caroline, but there was still tonight and tomorrow to deal with.

Confound the woman! She had to take the girl in. Certainly the duchess would see the impropriety of turning her away at this hour.

Pommy must have read his thoughts. "I shall not stay for a moment if she does not want me. I'll simply ask you to take me to an inn."

The thought that came to him then was so horrendous that he nearly missed the gates to Edgecumbe Manor.

Suppose he were forced to take Miss Fiske to a public inn in this neighborhood, where he was known, and pay her shot.

The fat would be in the fire indeed were Miss Anilee Mortimer to get wind of it.

She might well cry off . . .

Justin turned suddenly thoughtful. No, he couldn't trade Miss Fiske's good name for his own benefit. What a pity!

9

Justin drove smartly through the stone gateposts onto a well-kept if modestly narrow drive that wound through a handsome woodland. No fallen branches cluttered the floor of the woods, and shrubs, seemingly growing haphazardly along the drive, were nonetheless not allowed to obscure vision.

Justin glanced at Pommy. Sharply he demanded, "What's amiss? You look odd."

In truth, she felt odd, and she did not know why. Her mother had driven along this drive, she thought, when she was Pommy's age. Suddenly it seemed as though her father, in giving her no affection, had denied any part in her. He had of course seen to her education, even to the point of bringing her into society, but he had done these things from a sense of duty and probably a wish to spite her grandmother. If the duchess chose to use her granddaughter as a weapon to score on her son-in-law, then Pommy was in for a rocky road.

In a moment they emerged from the woodland into a spacious clearing, dotted sparsely with ornamental shrubs. In the center of the open space stood a house in the Georgian style, built of mellow Dorset stone. The architect had

designed the building in such perfect proportions as to give
an untrue impression of a small country cottage.

Pommy was overcome. She was here at last. While she
did not know whether her stay would be long or a matter
of a few minutes, at the moment all her doubts were forgotten.

This was a house her mother knew when she was a girl.
Pommy was disappointed. She did not know what she
expected, but surely dukes lived in a more lavish style than
this?

"Is this my grandmother's house?"

Justin was amused. "Did you expect a mansion like Chats-
worth? I believe the present duke's own seat, Woodburn,
is an impressive pile of stones without style." He stopped
short, remembering he was speaking to a member of the
duke's family, even though only distantly related. "The duke
lives in Derbyshire."

Justin did not tell her that his own Lisle Court, only a
couple of miles from here, was larger than Woodburn.

"This manor," Justin explained, "is the duchess's own,
given her by her father, I understand. Her grace told my
mother once that her entire life had been a misery and a
burden—I think her exact words—and she was, removing
here, in a sense retiring to a hermitage."

"How sad!"

Noting Pommy's sympathetic expression, he added,
"Don't waste your pity on her. She is not suffering greatly."

The hermitage, if that was how the duchess truly regarded
her home, was certainly not neglected. No weed dared to
grow in the flower beds, just now coming into early bloom.
The gravel drive had been raked recently. The window
frames and other wooden trim were freshly painted.

And for good measure, a boy appeared promptly from
somewhere to take charge of the horses and vehicle.

Justin handed the reins over and came to Pommy's side. He reached up to help her down. At least the duchess herself had not come storming out to repel invaders—yet!

The late-afternoon sun cast long shadows over the lawns. High in the trees a bird chirped occasionally, and along the road they had just left a horse and squeaky wagon could be heard. There was no sound of human inhabitants. Even the stable boy had not spoken a word.

Pommy whispered, "This house belongs to Sleeping Beauty."

"Frightened?"

"A little. No, that's not true. I am frightened to death."

"Don't be. I'll stay to support you."

His hand under her elbow, he propelled her toward the entrance. As they reached the bottom step, the door opened silently inward.

It was not a gnome who opened the door as Pommy half-expected, but a human butler in smart maroon livery. Old, bent, and obviously slow-moving, the man peered near-sightedly at the callers.

Justin searched his childhood memory for the name of the ancient servant. Strawn, that was it. He had thought the man dead long since.

Surely the man would not recognize him, thought Justin. How many years had it been since he came to call on the duchess?

Warily, lest the old butler sustain a damaging shock, Justin spoke from the bottom of the three entrance steps.

"Strawn, isn't it? I'm delighted to see you again. I should not be surprised if you have entirely forgotten me. I'm Justin Harcourt, from Lisle Court."

The old man's face crumpled in obvious relief. There's a gentleman for you, thought Strawn, don't leave you high and dry trying to remember a name you haven't thought of for ten years. Although to say truth, he amended, names of long ago come clearer to me now than yesterday's.

"Ah, yes, of course, sir. Young Master Justin. And Miss Caroline too, of course."

Justin took pity on him. "Miss Caroline is still in London, Strawn. And I am called Rutledge now, since my father died two years ago."

"Ah, yes, my lord. To be sure, her grace will be pleased to see you, my lord." Again glancing at Pommy, he added uncertainly, "And lady."

Strawn stepped back, opening the door wider in invitation. Justin urged Pommy up the steps, and they both stepped into the foyer. The pleasantly domestic aroma of beeswax and hothouse blooms came strongly to Pommy.

"How is her grace?" Justin asked. "I hope she is well and receiving guests today. I've brought someone to see her."

"Have you, my lord? Her grace don't get many visitors, out of the way as we are now. She'll be most pleased."

Strawn observed Pommy closely. "What name shall I say, my lord? For the lady, that is?"

He took a step closer, the better to aid his failing vision. Then, to the astonishment of both visitors, the man's color visibly drained away, leaving the wrinkled old face pale as parchment. He gave a kind of gabbling noise on an indrawn breath, a sound that Pommy translated surprisingly as "Goddlemighty!"

Justin leapt to catch the man before he fell to the floor. He could feel the trembling in Strawn's thin arm and cursed himself for bringing such a shock to the old man. Clearly the duchess had few visitors, and it was small wonder the frail butler found their arrival something of a strain.

But Strawn was recovering rapidly. However, he refused to look again at Pommy. As though he already knows he'll have to put me out in the road, she thought unhappily, and can't face me. He thinks of me as a disagreeable chore, like drowning kittens, probably.

But he looked so ill!

"Strawn," she exclaimed, "what is it? What's amiss?"

Pommy's light voice, while not loud, had good carrying qualities. Her words, spoken to the butler, drifted across the foyer, through a door at the back, and into the salon where the duchess sat.

Her grace, seated in her favorite chair by a window that looked out on a side lawn and a rose arbor, was not aware of her visitors. At the moment, she stared inimically at a piece of embroidery in her hands as though she expected an apology from it. Never had she been interested in needlework. Her governess at the time—whatever her name was— had informed her that a lady could be distinguished from the commonalty by the exquisite grace of her needlework. Young Lady Eleanor had voiced her opinion in one word: "Pooh!" She had never changed her mind.

But time hung heavy on her hands now, and in a kind of desperation she had resurrected from an old trunk in the attic this piece of material that she believed was to have been a chair cover.

She put the threaded needle into the cloth and in sudden revulsion wadded up the cloth and threw it with violence into a far corner.

It was then that she heard a female voice in the foyer where none should be. A visitor? She certainly hoped so. Strawn might not know what to do with a caller. She reached for her cane, pulled herself up, and moved, surprisingly quickly, toward the door.

Her butler was old. Indeed, he had served her father, and while he grew old and doddering now, she kept him on, finding no overt fault with him, but unobtrusively providing someone to assist him. That someone was clearly derelict in duty.

She advanced a few steps into the foyer. She took in the situation at a glance. Her sagging butler was being supported by a young man she knew. That cleft chin and the Harcourt eyebrows were an unmistakable stamp of identity. She had heard that Lord Rutledge was about to be married, and she supposed he had dutifully brought his affianced bride to Edgecumbe Manor to be presented to her.

"Young Justin," she crowed in happy recognition. "You've neglected me these years, sir."

"Your grace."

"But I suppose I should be grateful that you've come to visit at last."

"I've been abroad, ma'am, or I should have been on your doorstep months since," he said gallantly. He turned to Pommy to introduce her.

Pommy knew her manners. She stepped forward and dropped a curtsy. "Ma'am, please forgive me for arriving on your doorstep, without a word of warning or inquiry—"

The duchess's silver-knobbed cane clattered noisily to the Italian tile floor. With a cry Pommy leapt forward as the duchess, having stared at her with open mouth and astonished eyes, collapsed limply in a faint.

"Justin . . ." cried Pommy.

Lord Rutledge wished with all his might that he had never come to Edgecumbe Manor, not with Miss Fiske in tow. He wished, in fact, that he had gone home from Brooks's the other evening in his own carriage, which in the ordinary way he should have done. He wished fervently that he had allowed the house he now knew to be inhabited by the Derwents— curse them!—to be robbed of all their valuables. Were he to have it to do over, he would have with equanimity seen the whole of the furnishings of the house carried out before his eyes. Incensed as he was to be subjected to such a scene as lay before him now, he ignored the truth that no one had attempted to rob the house at all.

Facts aside, Justin had never expected to be standing in the foyer of an old and valued friend of his late mother's—a lady, moreover, who was their nearest neighbor—watching people swoon away and lie as though dead on the floor.

Never in a million years would he have come here had he known the outcome.

Pommy brought him sharply back to the present. "Stop mooning away, Justin. Strawn can't lift my grandmother. Do you come and help."

Strawn straigthened abruptly and made room for Lord Rutledge. He stared in wild surmise at the young lady, who coolly ordered his lordship about as though he were a footman.

"Lift her—gently!—and take her into that room. Strawn, there is a sofa there? I'll bring her cane."

Grandmother, she had said. Strawn nodded to himself. That was it, then.

Justin thought he knew the duchess rather well. However, he realized suddenly that he had known her personally only as a purveyor of sweets to a young boy, always hungry, and not as adult to adult.

While part of his mind searched for an answer to the riddle of why their arrival should result, almost before they had spoken, in the entire household lying about in inexplicable fainting spells, he responded dutifully to Pommy's instruction.

He picked up the duchess. She weighed no more than a feather, he thought. Perhaps her bones were hollow, like a bird's. He laid her down on an elegant Regency sofa, all white and gold, and looked around him.

The room had not changed since he had last been there.

He even remembered the covered glass dish on the table against the wall. He was tempted to lift the lid and look. Perhaps there were still some sugared almonds in it.

For the next several minutes he was hard-put to keep out of the way. Pommy had asked for a maid and some restorative remedies, particularly specifying brandy, but Strawn himself returned bearing a tray with cups and saucers and a teapot. Pommy left off chafing her grandmother's hands and coaxed the lady to open her eyes, and then to sip hot India tea that smelled strongly alcoholic.

While Pommy's hands moved efficiently in nursing her grandmother, her mind was in such a muddle. She had expected, perhaps, anger at her presumption in coming unbidden to the manor. Or dismay, possibly, at the unexpected appearance of a hobbledehoy—Cousin Lydia's word—claiming kinship. The possibility of her grandmother being completely revolted by the sight of her had also occurred to her.

But not this!

"Don't fuss, child," said her grace, finally sitting up straight. "Give me a moment to finish this tea." With a final swallow, she put her fragile china cup and saucer into Pommy's hands and waved the tea cart away.

Strawn leaned heavily on the cart as he removed it, and Justin, amused, saw that once he was outside the room, he emptied the teapot into an unused cup and tossed the brandy-laced tea back in one gulp.

It was clear enough that a shock of no mean order had come to the residents of Edgecumbe Manor.

"I'm such a fool," said the duchess. "I never fainted in my entire life to this point. Except, of course, on purpose. Child, have you learned yet how best to faint? Sometimes a swoon can be most diplomatic. But this was totally unsuspected." She gestured. "Come and sit next to me."

Pommy obeyed.

The duchess studied her face, feature by feature, and at length nodded. "My dear," she said in a voice that contained neither disapproval nor indifference, "apologies are certainly in order. You must indulge me for a few moments, because you must know I am not accustomed to making explanations, especially of such disgraceful behavior as I have just exhibited."

"Please, your grace—" Pommy murmured.

"My only excuse is that you startled me. Indeed you did. I vow I have never been so shocked in my life, even when . . . But pooh to that."

Pommy twisted so that she could watch her grandmother's face. She saw an old woman, still handsome in an autocratic way. She must have been a raving beauty in her youth. She was tiny and delicately thin. She was nearly as fragile as one of her own porcelain cups. Could this be the lady with the soft hands she thought she remembered? She was not sure, but her grandmother's musical voice seemed to waken a long-forgotten echo.

Justin felt reassured by the sight of the duchess and her granddaughter side by side on the sofa. Pommy's immediate future—at least this night—seemed secure.

"Your grace, I had not thought the pair of us were so ugly as to be a danger to the public," he said, gently teasing the old lady. "For you must know that Strawn was as close to collapse as may be. Of course, he must be old and feeble, so that my appearing suddenly after some years away was too much for him."

"My dear boy," said the duchess dryly, "pray do not flatter yourself. Both my butler and I could sustain the shock of seeing you with—I shall not say indifference, for truly I am fond of you, Justin—but with reasonable poise."

She reached to touch Pommy's folded hands before continuing. "However, you will not think it wonderful that we were both overset. Strawn, you must know, has been with me since I was first married to the duke. Rest his soul." The last remark, thought Justin, lacked the ring of true piety. "But, look there"—she directed—"and you will understand."

With a gesture of a graceful hand wearing, thought Pommy, all the diamond rings in Middlesex, the duchess indicated the opposite wall of her salon.

The salon was not a large room. On the indicated wall was a fireplace with an Adam mantel, and before the hearth a pair of old-fashioned bergère chairs facing each other.

The painting above the fireplace dominated the salon. Their first attention on entering the room had been the restoring of the duchess to herself. But once they saw the portrait, they could not turn away from it.

The artist had portrayed a lovely young lady. Her deep-red hair was dressed in an outdated style, and the lighting in the portrait had been cunningly contrived to turn the glorious color of it into a rich mahogany.

The painted young lady seemed to look with speaking gray eyes at Justin with amusement. He had seen just that look before, and not long since either. "Good God, it's Pommy."

"You see?" the duchess said in quiet triumph.

"But how could it be?"

"Don't be foolish, Justin," Pommy said in an odd voice. "It is my mother. I know, because my father has a miniature of her in his study. Not so fine as this, of course."

"Of course it isn't," snorted the duchess. "Julia sat to Raeburn for this. But you see, my dear, when I saw you, I thought for a moment that my daughter had returned to me, even though she has been dead these nineteen years."

Pommy said shyly, "I'm sorry, ma'am. I did not know I resembled her so closely."

Justin said irritably, "How could you not know, if you had a portrait."

"But I only saw it a few times, when I was much younger. My father kept it locked away in a desk drawer."

"Just like him," the duchess said bitterly. "He's locked you away as well. Tell me, child, what do they call you?"

"My name is Melpomene."

"I know that, and a more barbarian name I never heard. He made sure I knew what name he had you christened. I suppose he thought it a kind of triumph, showing me how little he thought of me. I told him his duty was to name you Julia for your mother. That would have been so much more suitable."

Justin found the conversation fascinating. Pommy had had such doubts about her reception by her grandmother, heretofore unknown to her, and yet here the two of them were gossiping like a pair of bosom friends.

Curiosity moved him. "But why Melpomene?"

"I was told it was intended that I be called Clio. But my mother died, so I became Melpomene."

"Clio, the Muse of History? I suppose that fits some wayward sense of logic. But Melpomene?"

"The Muse of Tragedy, of course," Pommy explained.

The duchess was appalled. "Do not tell me he intended to beget all the muses?"

Justin laughed. "No man would cheerfully anticipate nine daughters, ma'am. Just think of it."

"I prefer not to. My Julia is better-off in her grave." But the duchess was moved to a reluctant smile. "I always said the man was mad. And where is he now?"

"In Greece, ma'am."

"You cannot persuade me, my dear, that you are truly called Mel-pom-en-e?"

"No, ma'am. Only by my father when he . . . No—that

is, when he is distressed with me." Justin was certain she started to say when he notices me. "Mostly I am called Pommy."

"Good God, that's worse."

Justin felt it was time to intervene. While he now had no fear that Pommy would be cut adrift, yet there were loose ends to be dealt with. For one, there was Pommy's escape from her legal though temporary guardian. For another, there was her engagement, by now announced officially in the *Gazette*. The duchess must be informed of possible complications, not to say disasters, that might arise.

"I am gratified, ma'am, that I need not attempt to persuade you that this young lady is your granddaughter. I anticipated you would require baptism certificates and many other documents to convince you that Pommy is not an impostor."

Pommy exclaimed, "I never thought of that."

"Her face is all the proof I need." Her grace's deep-blue eyes kindled. "Thanks to that idiot father of hers, I don't know my own granddaughter. I should have been acquainted with her long since. He could easily have sent her to me anytime. If he has finally given in to what decent feelings he might have, he could have let me know. I should have given you a better reception, my dear."

Justin and Pommy spoke together. "But he hasn't—"

The duchess said after a moment, "No? Then Pommy can tell me all about it. The tale should at least beguile a long summer evening."

Pommy smiled broadly. At least for some time—for summer evenings to come—she would have a home. And maybe if she had to come into society, her grandmother might manage the whole of it. But for now, Pommy was content.

When she again paid heed to her surroundings, the duchess was quizzing Justin. "Young man, I have heard you are about to marry. And not a minute before time. Your father's been gone two years now, and no heir coming after you. A shame. But I hope you will not tell me you have offered for my granddaugther?''

Justin turned frostly. "No," he said forcefully, "I have not.''

''Excellent,'' said her grace, blandly ignoring the heat with which he rejected the idea of marrying Pommy. ''Just as well, for I shall expect to be consulted about my granddaughter's marriage. Not that you are not a prime catch for somebody.'' She laughed. ''No need to show your temper with me, you know. I've known you since you were in leading strings, and you can't intimidate me with that scowl.''

Justin considered himself justifiably irritated. Indeed, it would not have been wonderful had he stalked out in high dudgeon. He had, the last forty-eight hours, been jolted far out of his ordinary ways, and he was sure he didn't like it. Although he had been unutterably bored with his days and nights in London, and even more been loath to contemplate his inevitable marriage, he was learning that abrupt change was not to his liking, either.

First had come the incident of the runaway young lady in the garden and his sister's shocked revelation of her identity. Then, swift on the heels of that possible scandal came the distasteful Watters episode and this wretched miss running away again.

A man ordinarily dignified and conscious of his station in life, Justin had been made to look the fool by the folk in the stagecoach.

What a shambles Pommy had made of his life. He was guilty of kidnapping a lady of quality—twice! Guilty of removing the girl from her lawful home, and certainly to appear with her, unchaperoned, in the wilds of Middlesex could not be admired by any of his friends. And yet . . .

And yet he had felt thoroughly alive these last few days as he had not since he could remember.

Now he remembered his dignity. He rose to leave. "They do not know I am coming at Lisle Court. It is getting dark and the moon will not rise till late. But, your grace, I think I should warn you that inquiries may be made for Pommy."

"Inquiries? What sort of inquiries?"

"I am not sure precisely. You may refer the officials to me if you wish." He smiled.

"Officials! Justin, I demand to know what you are talking about?"

"It is simple, ma'am. They may be asking about Pommy. You see, I kidnapped her off the stagecoach, and the other passengers may be anxious about her."

After he had gone, the duchess stared at Pommy in wild speculation. What kind of wayward miss had Julia's daughter become?

"Well, Pommy," she said at last, "it appears we will have sufficient to talk about for some time." Her eyes twinkled and she smiled. At least, she decided, life wouldn't be dull as ditch water anymore.

10

The next morning, after Pommy had been restored by a hearty supper and a dreamless sleep in a bedroom she was told had been her mother's, she was herself again.

And so was the duchess.

Born Lady Eleanor Cherwyn, of the great family of that name whose branches spread from Hertfordshire into Buckinghamshire and Middlesex, she had grown up intelligent and aware of her own importance in the scheme of things. Her strong will, however, was not sufficient to remove her from the necessity of marrying to oblige her family, as the delicate phrase went. She had not liked the duke from the start, but it was not her doing that only one child was born of the marriage, and that one a mere female.

To the regret of none who knew him, the Duke of Woodburn succumbed to a violent fever while visiting, without his duchess, in Portugal. In due course the new duke, from a distant branch of the family, arrived at the traditional ducal country seat of Woodburn to find the famous and massive set of Georgian silver missing, as well as some paintings of small size but great value.

The dowager duchess had left a message for her husband's successor that she had removed her household permanently to her own property of Edgecumbe Manor, scorning the Woodburn dower house and taking her own possessions and certain objects she liked and had grown accustomed to having about her. After a dozen fruitless attempts to point out to her her clear duty to return Woodburn property to its rightful owner, the new duke confessed himself beaten.

Exceedingly well-bred and educated, she was a woman of great charm and, in her day, influence. After her daughter Julia's marriage and subsequent death in childbirth, the dowager duchess immured herself in the country cottage she owned in Middlesex. She considered Edgecumbe Manor to be a small house symbolic of her retirement from the social world, since it contained a mere twenty-six rooms, requiring a bare skeleton of a staff, pared to the bone and numbering only eighteen.

She had lost heart for society after Julia's death, but now, delighted to have her granddaughter under her roof for the first time, she felt the embers of that former life stirring within her. Only a small breath of air would be required to fan into flame her penchant for excitement, intrigue, and—truth to tell—overwhelming management of the affairs of other people.

She regarded her granddaughter over the breakfast table. "I do not perfectly understand how it is that you arrived on my doorstep. I must apologize again for both Strawn and myself. What a welcome we gave you. But you must never doubt that I am overjoyed to have you with me."

"Oh, no, ma'am. You're so very kind. And not at all what I expected."

The duchess's lips tightened. "I am sure not. Your father must have described me as a wicked witch, with claws instead of fingers and my hair all hissing snakes like Medusa."

Since her father's description of his mother-in-law, on the one occasion when Pommy, greatly daring, had asked about her, was recognizably close to that, Pommy found nothing to say.

"But how was it that Justin knew you were on the Bath coach?"

"He told me he was not sure that I was. But since he knew I wished to come here, he took a gamble and came after me."

"But how did he know you wished to come to me? Did you meet him at an affair in London? I know—at Almack's."

"Oh, no, ma'am," Pommy said, shocked. "I am not out, and I probably shall never be allowed inside the door. There was to be a ball to introduce me, you know, but after I had been in Berkeley Square a few weeks, Cousin Lydia told me I must give up any idea of coming into society."

"Good God, why?"

"Because she said I was so harum-scarum that I would disgrace her, no matter how she tried to mold me. To bring me up to the mark. She said that only her son, Frederick, would be willing to marry me and that was merely because of my fortune."

"Indeed," said the duchess faintly. "My granddaughter, ill-bred?"

Pommy applied herself to the plate of fresh hot muffins that Strawn brought. "Butter from the farm, miss," he said proudly, "and honey from our own bees."

"Delicious! I can't think why I am eating so much."

"I should judge that woman," said her grace dryly, "did not even feed you decently."

After Strawn left, the duchess renewed the attack. "Why did she say you were beyond help? Your manners are charming, and I could not wish for a more delightful granddaughter. I must inform you that I consider Lady Derwent a great booby, as well as being more than a shade common. Pooh to her opinion! Did your father not provide governesses?"

"Oh, yes, ma'am, he did. And even Miss Horne, my last governess, said I was quite *comme il faut*. But London ways seem so much different, and even unfathomable. For instance, I rode in the park—a really lovely place, I thought—but Cousin Lydia gave me a great scold."

The duchess was beginning to take Pommy's measure. "You galloped in Hyde Park."

"You heard about that?"

"I do not need to be told. Any girl brought up in the country, and seeing those long vistas ahead of her, must of course gallop. But only once."

"Oh, yes, I dared not do that again. Such a peal as Cousin Lydia rang over me."

"My dear, you will oblige me by refraining from calling that woman cousin. But surely that small indiscretion was not sufficient reason to cancel your ball?"

Pommy, for the first time since she left Beechknoll for the city, felt accepted. The duchess, while she might not approve of all that Pommy had done—and she had heard only an incident or two as yet—regarded her with a warmth in her eyes that cheered Pommy more than anything in her life so far.

"No, ma'am. I think it was the dog."

By now the duchess was engrossed in the unfolding saga of Pommy's descent on London. "Pour me some coffee, my dear, and tell me about the dog."

The incident of the dog nearly overset the duchess. By no stretch of her humanitarian instincts could she condone a totally scandalous foray down St. James's Street, even though Pommy had ventured only a dozen steps into forbidden territory—where all the clubmen sat in bow windows ogling any female within sight, or so it was said—to rescue a wounded puppy.

Very reluctantly she had to agree with Lady Derwent. But

even so it was not a sufficient social sin to blast the girl's chances for a reasonable match, especially when Pommy was not out yet and it could be assumed she was not readily recognized. Her fortune, which her grace had previously taken pains to investigate privately, was sufficient to overcome a worse scandal than anything she had heard so far. If there were additional and more vital lapses on Pommy's part, she did not wish to hear about them.

But there were things she must know. "Did Justin say that you were engaged to Lady Derwent's son, whatever his name is?"

"Yes, ma'am. His name is Frederick Watters, from her first marriage, you know." She added shyly, "I believe I still am betrothed. They were to put it in the paper yesterday."

"She announced your betrothal to her son? And you aren't in society yet?"

"Well, I did not think it precisely the thing myself. But I loathe the man so much, and I know I will not marry him, so I did not see that it made a great difference. Besides, Papa had agreed to it."

"Oh, had he?"

"Cous—that is, Lady Derwent told me she had written asking his permission. I did ask Papa before he took me to London if I could not come up here to you."

The duchess sat very still. "And he said?"

Pommy's chin trembled. The reality of her situation came to her with force. "He s-said you did not want me. And I came up here without even a by-your-leave." Tears stood in her eyes.

The duchess spoke vehemently. "Fool he is, and always was. I regret to tell you that your father is a liar, and what's more, a vindictive one."

Pommy did not disagree. "Then I can stay?"

"Where else in the civilized world would my grand-daughter stay but with me?" It was a grand remark, and Pommy's smile of relief was a joy to behold, thought her grace. But enough emotion for the moment. "Justin said he took you off the stage? Somehow I thought he would have more care for his consequence."

"Well, you see, it was because I hadn't gone back to Lady Playre's when I escaped from Frederick . . ."

It took most of the morning before the duchess believed she had at last a clear picture of her granddaughter's most recent forty-eight hours. While she could wish that Pommy had been a trifle more conventional, she also realized that Pommy had inherited a good bit of her waywardness and determination from the duchess herself.

"Pray do not think," Pommy explained, "that he had any vicious reasons to kidnap me. It was merely that he felt responsible for me."

"And why would he?"

"If he had let me go at the start, not interfered when I left the house that night, he wouldn't have had to take me to Lady Playre and I would not have had to run away from Frederick in the carriage. Because I would have taken the stage that next morning and I would have already been here."

Unless robbed, murdered, stolen away by men of evil intent, thought the duchess, and sent up a prayer of gratitude for Justin's timely intervention.

One phrase of Justin's came to her now. What had he meant of "officials"? Surely this Watters idiot would not have put his problems into the hands of the law? Law was all well and good, but not when applied to the duchess or, by extension, any of her family.

"I suppose Justin did not inform Lady Derwent or her son of his intention to find you and bring you to me?"

"I do not think so."

"Well, then, I suppose I may expect the runners in my driveway at any moment."

Pommy was distressed. "Oh, ma'am, do you think so?"

The duchess, her eyes alight with anticipation, beamed on her granddaughter. "I certainly hope so. I cannot think how young—Watters, did you say?—came to be so common as to call in the Bow Street Runners to find his affianced bride. But I should take into consideration the extreme vulgarity of his mother's breeding. No lady of my acquaintance has ever had to deal with the runners. Quite a diversion, don't you think?"

The dowager duchess clearly entertained an abiding and undiscriminating contempt for the whole of Sir Arthur Fiske's kin. From her own short acquaintance with her father's cousin, Pommy could join in heartily. She knew it was not proper to think ill of her father, and for the most part she nourished a small spark of uncritical affection for him.

But where Pommy's only way of dealing with her father's relation was to run away from them, she suspected her grandmother of cultivating more belligerent prospects.

"Where are your clothes, my dear?"

"I left them in Berkeley Square. Cousin Lydia had had some gowns made for me, but I did not like them and of course I could not carry them with me."

"Certainly they would all be in dreadful taste. You must be properly dressed now, especially with the Rutledge wedding coming along. There will be parties and outings. We will entertain, and you must help me decide whether we give a country dance or an elegant luncheon."

Pommy had fallen silent. In her mind Justin moved and even smiled at her. She had known from the beginning that he was about to be betrothed, the wedding to follow quickly. But it occurred to her that, supposing she were to be a bride, she would wish her bridegroom to appear, if not jubilant, at least happier at the prospect of their approaching union. She had seen no sign of anything but reluctance on the part of the bridegroom in question. In fact, she thought, she had seen just such an expression in the eyes of a hare caught in a snare.

A memory came sharply to her: she and Justin crouching in the shrubbery, his cloak covering them both, while his fiancée and her parents left Lady Playre's party. His words at that moment were not those of a man deeply in love. "I forgot her completely," he had exclaimed.

How could a man forget the woman he wanted to marry? Although nothing to the point had been said in her hearing, she believed it possible he did not want to marry Miss Mortimer at all. For a moment, she pitied Justin, but only for a moment. Surely any man of any value would take charge of his own destiny.

Her grandmother's voice brought her back to herself.

"My dear, what do you think of Justin?"

"He seems very nice. He was kind to me."

As an accolade, her remarks fell short. But there was something in the tone in which they were spoken that caught the duchess's curiosity. She expected that any green girl—as she must admit her granddaughter was—would be awed by the elegant gentleman who had temporarily taken charge of her. But this remote voice was not that of a gushing girl.

She had come upon something of significance, the dowager thought, but what Pommy's reaction meant, she could not fathom. Perhaps Pommy was truly indifferent to Justin. Or perhaps she was already half in love with the man.

She had no objection herself to marrying off her granddaughter to Lord Rutledge. He was a fine catch, he was a near neighbor, and in despising Watters he showed excellent judgment. It would also do the duchess's heart good to forestall whatever plans Sir Arthur had made for his daughter.

There was only one snag: Justin was all but formally betrothed to Anilee Mortimer. The girl and her parents were coming up for a family fortnight, and the betrothal would be announced sometime during this visit.

All these arrangements had been made. Lady Playre had entertained for them in London only three nights ago. The match was as good as done in the eyes of all of London.

The duchess gave her opinion of all these elaborate plans, but not aloud. "Pooh to them!"

11

The next few days fairly flew by for Pommy. Seamstresses came, measured, displayed bolts of gorgeous fabrics and yards and yards of lace and ribbons and braids imported from Paris, and set to work.

Callers came nearly every afternoon, word having flown on the wind that the duchess's estranged granddaughter had, like the Prodigal, come home.

But of all the things that the duchess had done for her, Pommy was perhaps most grateful for her instructions to Asbury, who managed the extensive farms belonging to Edgecumbe Manor.

"I want her to have free rein of the manor, Asbury. Let her get the London smoke out of her lungs." And Sir Arthur's kin, added the duchess silently, off the dear child's mind.

Asbury was a man of no more than medium height, heavy in the shoulders so as to appear stocky. His face was weathered to a nut-brown outdoor color, and when he laughed, crinkles appeared at the corners of his eyes.

Asbury provided a mare for Pommy to ride and a groom to accompany her whenever she chose to ride out on the public ways. The manager himself often accompanied her as she explored the farms of the manor. She had had the oversight of her father's estate, rather larger than Edgecumbe, since she was in her early teens. While Sir Arthur and his manager had made the decisions, Pommy had been entrusted with overseeing the day-to-day operations.

She was knowledgeable about farming, but Asbury knew much about the new methods of agriculture coming from some of the modern schools in Germany and Austria. She won his allegiance at once by her genuine interest, and he told Mrs. Asbury that the young miss was slap up to the mark and didn't have her head filled with all that city nonsense.

One day soon after she had come, Asbury rode out with her in a different direction from before.

"You ought to see just where her grace's butts and bounds be, so you don't accidentally trespass on the neighbors. There's Lord Rutledge to the east there, but we'll come back that way. There's something I want to show you, last thing today. We'll start the other direction."

They trotted from the stables on a lane leading to the west. Once past the house, they turned toward the public road that passed the gates. From the entrance the stone wall marked the edge of the estate as far as the western boundary. At that point, they turned right on what might once have been called the West Riding. They trotted easily on a lane too narrow for farm wagons and rode for some distance.

"Vivyans' land butts up against Edgecumbe the whole west edge," he told her.

He pointed out the various crops as they rode. The fields were broad and rolling gently, rising slightly toward the north. At the end of this lane, they came to the river, the northern boundary. The stream was not a wide one, but the current was strong.

The fourth side of the manor's land was separated from Lord Rutledge's by a wide dirt road that was carried over the stream by a sturdy bridge. "The wagons come this way," explained Asbury. "May be you remember passing the gates as you came? That's where the other end of the road comes out."

Pommy vaguely recalled a poor set of gates, in good repair but not grand, as Justin drove her a week ago. She had paid them no heed at the time, but now she learned that those gates gave entrance to this wagon road, which was used by both Rutledge and Edgecumbe farmers.

Pommy and Asbury had made slow progress as he talked about the fields he loved. It was getting late, but there was still something he wished to show her.

Turning onto the road in the direction of the house, they cantered slowly toward home. They passed a small house along the edge of the road. It was a building well enough in repair, although the thatch had lifted over the winter and needed beating back and the moss removed. A pair of small children stood by the side of the road in front of the shack and waved at them.

Asbury pulled up and Pommy followed his example. The children stared shyly at Pommy, and she smiled encouragingly at them.

"These are Proggs," Asbury told her. For a wild moment, she thought he meant the little girls were of another species, and at first she could believe it. Thin and brown from the sun, they peered out at her from under thatches of uncombed hair. Their eyes were a startling blue, and brightly curious. It was clear they knew who she was.

Had Pommy been ignorant of country ways, she might have thought the children were neglected and starving. But she looked across the field and saw workers in the field, moving along the rows and swinging their sticks and weed hooks. Without doubt their parents were among them.

Addressing the older of the two, she said, "Your name is Progg?"

"Yes, miss."

"And what is your first name?"

Shyly, the girl hung her head. But she answered, and Pommy could make out the words. "They call me Molly, and her is Sal."

"You live here in this house?"

Nervously they rolled those astonishingly blue eyes toward Asbury. "No, miss," Molly said, and Sal at the same moment, said, "Yes, miss."

Asbury was nettled. "What they mean, Miss Pommy, is that they are not supposed to be living here, because the house is to be torn down and a new one built for them. But they won't leave and let me get on with it."

Molly seemed the more confident of the two. "And Pa says," she told Asbury, "we need it till after malting time."

Sal added explanation. "Rain."

"It's true," Asbury said grudgingly, lest Pommy think he was not aggressive in her grace's interest. "It's a close shelter in case of bad weather."

"Of course," agreed Pommy. "Are the storms severe here?"

After a bit she waved good-bye to the children, and she and Asbury continued on their tour of the estate. They had not far to go. Ahead was a dark smudge across the horizon, which she knew to be the home wood.

"And supposing you yourself, Miss Pommy, should get caught by weather or something, I'll show you where you can get shelter, you and your horse, for you'll likely not be walking. The lightning is sometimes fearful, and I've known horses to run to their deaths from fright. Not that Star there is skittish, but better to get inside when you can."

Some short distance ahead before they reached the home wood stood a snug barn. "Forage we keep in there and some tools. But there's room for horse and rider, or even two. You see, it's on her grace's side of the road, and you'd not be trespassing to use it. Not that Lord Rutledge is a high stickler for the law. Now his father . . ."

They dismounted and he showed her how to undo the latch and open the door. Inside, all was dark and shadowy, and a good smell of dried grass and dirt and hay came to her.

Again they set forth, this time on the last leg of the tour. She felt the mare's rhythm lifting her gently, and the breeze of their passing cooled her cheek. This happiness was worth all the trouble she had had in getting here.

The day's pleasures were not over. They approached the woods that marked the end of this road. The half-mile belt of trees bordered the public road, providing privacy and protection for Edgecumbe Manor.

Emerging from an obscure side lane to their left came a magnificent stallion, groomed to a high sheen the color of a new-minted copper coin. But it was the rider who caught Pommy's attention.

She smiled broadly. "Justin! What a surprise?"

She felt her cheeks burning. What a stupid thing to say! It could not be unexpected to see a landowner riding on his own acres. No wonder Cousin Lydia thought she was unschooled.

He spoke to her, but she could not afterward remember a syllable he uttered.

Asbury came to her rescue. "I was just showing Miss Pommy the tree where Miss Julia used to read."

"Tree?" Justin said.

"The old beech," Asbury explained. "When Miss Julia was out of sorts with her grace, she used to bring a book and climb up in that tree. No one from the house knew where she was. But I did.''

"I remember this tree very well. But I understood,'' said Justin, ''that her grace moved here only after her daughter died.''

"Aye, a matter of some twenty years maybe. But she used to come here often before then, brought Miss Julia with her. A little vacation from the duke, she used to call it.''

Soon Asbury suggested they move on. It was not his place to do so, he knew, but there were chores at the house and his farm books needed work; he was already, because of last week's storms, badly behind in his work.

"Go on, Asbury,'' said Justin. ''I'll see that Miss Pommy gets home safely.''

Asbury turned back the way they had come and put his horse into a canter. Belatedly Justin realized that no groom was in sight, and he and Pommy were again alone. His standards of civility seemed, since he had met Pommy, to have vanished as though they never were. His best remedy was to get her back to the manor as soon as possible.

He turned to urge her toward the house. To his surprise she had dismounted and tied Star to a nearby sapling. She was looking up at the great copper beech with a glint in her eye that filled him with foreboding.

"What are you up to now?'' he said, irritated. ''I should get you home.''

"To think my mother climbed this tree before I was born.''

"She could hardly climb it afterward.'' He was sorry for his words the instant they were spoken. He had forgotten for the moment that Pommy's mother had died giving birth to her.

But Pommy seemed not to have heard him. ''I wonder . . .'' she said, touching the trunk.

"Pommy, you're not going to try—"

She was indeed. She jumped up to get a hold on a sturdy lower branch and hung there for a moment. She was faced now with a dilemma that was new to her. At home she would simply have pulled herself up, having first hitched up her skirt above her knees, and hooked a knee across the branch. After that, it would be easy.

But here was a gentleman, watching her with some amusement, and she simply dared not take the next step. Her skirt must remain stretched demurely to her ankles, and acrobatic maneuvers must be sternly suppressed. Reluctantly she let herself drop to the ground.

When she caught his eye, he grinned broadly. "What stopped you? Even I can believe you are capable of climbing that tree. Anyone who has practiced on a trellis in Berkeley Square should have no trouble with a beech in Middlesex."

Suddenly she felt comfortable with him. She did not know how it was—perhaps they had been through too many unconventional incidents together. At any rate, she laughed. "The trellis was not the first object I ever climbed down, or up. I must tell you there is not a tree at Beechknoll I have not scaled."

"But why? You did not need a vacation from the duke."

Her expression turned sober. "No. My father." Her cares, at bay for a few days while her grandmother cosseted her, came back with a rush. There was Frederick, there was Cousin Lydia, there was the betrothal, and there was her father, who had the final disposition of Pommy's future. She turned her face away lest Justin see her distress.

But he had seen it. After a moment, he said, "I seem to say all the wrong things today. What can I do? Help you up the tree? Help you to mount? Go home and cover myself with sackcloth and ashes?"

"Ridiculous!" She had to laugh. "You always put me in

a better humor," she told him. "Unless, of course, you make me angry."

"Which I seem to do before I know what I am about," he said ruefully.

He was afoot, ready to help her mount again. "Are you happy here? Does her grace frighten you?"

The concern in his eyes was like a caress from a gentle hand. It was strange that of all the people she knew, only this man she had met briefly and under singular circumstances used that tone of voice with her. Her grandmother was brisk and bracing, her father spoke with the utmost indifference, Cousin Lydia whined. And only this man had the power to bring tears to her eyes.

"She treats me very well," Pommy said in response to his question. "It was the right thing for me to do, to be sure, even though I did have my doubts."

"I should think you must find it dull here in the country."

"Oh, my, no. My grandmother knows everyone, I think, and we have had a constant stream of visitors."

He longed to know whether pursuers from Bow Street had arrived on the duchess's doorstep, but he feared to inquire lest Pommy begin to worry. He believed she was completely capable of deciding she was bringing trouble to her grandmother, and running away again. Stooping with hands cupped at his knee, he helped her into the saddle.

They rode together as far as the Edgecumbe stable.

"My sister is arriving day after tomorrow. She will call on her grace."

"Delightful! I shall be glad to see her."

After he had seen her safely into the hands of Darnly, the head groom, Justin rode back through the woods and stopped at the great beech tree. He remembered that tree. Any boy would. He himself had climbed up into its branches, with a book or not, and secreted himself in an illusion of prefect privacy. The tree could be what one willed it to be. Primarily in his own youth, he remembered, it was the crow's nest on the treasure-filled *Golden Hind*, the sharp-eyed lookout, one Justin Harcourt, catching first sight of England after three years, as the brave little ship came close-hauled up the channel. Would he ever have sons to enjoy the same fine dreaming hours?

While Pommy took pleasure in the farms and riding free along the farm lanes, the dowager duchess was enjoying herself, in her own way, for the first time in years. In fact, not since she had removed the family silver from Woodburn had she felt such a surge of satisfaction.

The new duke had given up the unequal quarrel before she was finished with their brisk and, on her side at least, libelous correspondence. Sir Arthur, too, had had the last word by the simple expedient of keeping her granddaughter immured and safe from her interference.

The truth was, her grace had run out of opponents.

Now, just before the duchess expired from severe boredom, came Pommy, bringing, as it were, life-saving opportunities and broad new vistas for the *intrigante*.

First was the undoubted pleasure of meeting her granddaughter and finding her a delightful child. When Pommy looked at her grandmother, gravely, her gray eyes as smoky as Julia's had been, the duchess felt her heart twist in her breast. How much the girl was like her mother! Not as stubborn as Julia, one hoped, and a good deal more sweet-natured, Pommy was all that the duchess could have wished for. Her grace found her manners charming. What could that Derwent woman have found fault with? What more could she want? The duchess concluded, rightly, that what that woman wanted was Pommy's fortune in her son's hands.

And that, vowed the duchess, would never come to pass.

One small thing that Lord Rutledge had hinted at when he had brought Pommy to her: that Edgecumbe Manor might receive a visit from Bow Street Runners. Justin had thought to shock her. On the contrary, she would, if necessary, stand in the drive at the gates in order not to miss them.

In her morning room, seated at her small French writing desk, she considered her next move. If Pommy's betrothal to Frederick Whatever-his-name-was indeed had been announced as Justin informed her, it must be rescinded at once.

She knew the girl must be presented to society, and not squirreled away in Lady Derwent's home. After all, Pommy was a duke's granddaughter, and her rank demanded the best. The duchess herself would bring Pommy out. She might even take a house for the Little Season. It was only May now—she had enough time to plan.

Shrewdly, the duchess realized that there would not be easy sailing ahead. Fortunately, Pommy's father was a world away, in Greece. Probably he was on one of those waterless islands with no mail coming in for months, and Pommy had said she did not expect him back in England before the winter.

A month for mail to go from Edgecumbe to the Aegean Sea, a month to return, supposing the man gave a groat for his daughter. Yes, the duchess decided, there was time enough to bring the girl into society and have her well-betrothed if not wed by the time Sir Arthur stirred himself.

In the meantime, she knew her legal position might be flawed. Sir Arthur had disposed of his daughter's custody, putting her into the hands of his cousin. The girl was at present not in that guardian's hands; therefore, the duchess had to admit, her father had a right to know where she was.

It was a happy circumstance that the duchess's moral obligation to tell Sir Arthur that his previously sequestered daughter had trusted her instincts and sought refuge at Edgecumbe coincided with her grace's wish to point out a few home truths to him.

She took pen in hand and addressed herself to the task.

After the purely formal salutations, required among civilized persons, she moved to the meat of her message.

"I cannot believe that a man of your education, specialized as it may be, would consider a woman as common as Lydia Derwent a suitable chaperone for a delicately nurtured female such as Melpomene."

Her grace spared a thought for the tanned Amazon riding Star as though she had been born on her back. And for the daring conspirator climbing down a trellis at midnight, riding on a public stage. Her pen moved up a line and underscored "delicately nurtured."

"The woman is a vulgar, greedy and quite grasping parasite. Her sole thought seems to be to provide a fortune for her loose screw of a son . . ."

Perhaps my slang is not quite up to date, thought her grace, since I have not been in society these several years. However, the meaning of her expressions was flawlessly clear.

"I have been told that you have given permission to the marriage between Melpomene and that feeble Watters boy. I can only conclude that your few remaining wits have been addled by the tropical sun. While I consider young Watters an entirely suitable son-in-law for you, and the least you deserve, I will not sacrifice my granddaughter for revenge, an emotion entirely too common for me to entertain."

She felt only a momentary twinge, not of conscience of course, but of apprehension that she was cutting it a bit too strong. Nonetheless, she changed not a word. One more paragraph . . .

"Since you are her father, even though you do not seem

to be cognizant of the responsibilities and privileges of that relationship, you have a . . .''

She brushed the top of the quill absently against her cheek. She meant to say ''legal right.'' After consideration, she considered it better not to mention the law in connection with Pommy, what with Bow Street Runners and the lot.

She finished swiftly. ''You have a right to know where she is. I am happy to inform you that she is safely here with me.''

With a sigh of pleasant duty accomplished, she sealed the letter and sent it under a cover to a friend in a high government position in London. He would know how to send the letter on to Greece. She hoped he would not hasten to get the letter on its way abroad. Perhaps she could count on its taking more than two months even to arrive at its destination.

The letter in only two days traveled the short distance to London and was delivered. Her grace's friend, curious as to why the duchess, who loathed Sir Arthur, was writing to him, balanced the letter in his hand for a moment.

He knew quite well that Sir Arthur Fiske was not in the Aegean. He had traveled, in fact, only as far as Rome. The eastern Mediterranean countries were, as usual, in a state of beligerency, most pronounced at the moment, and all traffic of English citizens in that direction had been halted.

Directing his cover letter to the ambassador in Rome, he sent her grace's letter on its way.

Happily for the duchess, he thought, her letter will arrive in a fortnight or less.

12

Lisle Court was presently in the throes of a domestic upset the like of which had not been seen for five years. At the time old Lord Rutledge was still domineeringly alive, and that occasion was the impending marriage of the daughter of the house, Miss Caroline Harcourt, to Gervase Quentin, Lord Playre.

Hibbert, the Lisle Court butler, was now faced with an event that he feared would tax his considerable, though very rusty, organizing talents. It was not every day that a country house the size of Lisle Court—some fifty rooms—was made ready to entertain a large house party, and one, moreover, that could change the lives of man and servant alike.

It was understood in the servants' hall that his lordship would announce his betrothal at some time in this fortnight, and the staff was agog to catch the first glimpse of the chosen lady. If the next Lady Rutledge were amiable, then the future of everyone in the house would likely be seen through a rosy haze. If she were not . . .

While Hibbert with determination maintained an optimistic outlook, especially in front of his staff, he regarded his lordship with some apprehension. Nothing of the happy bridegroom about Lord Rutledge, thought Hibbert, and indeed one might think his lordship had less interest in his coming nuptials than he had in a new foal in the stables.

In the way of servants, those at Edgecumbe Manor had lost little time in informing those at Lisle Court of the arrival of her grace's granddaughter, and in particular the manner of her coming. Alone with Lord Rutledge. In a curricle, and not a closed coach to be sure, but nonetheless shocking behavior on the part of the quality. And a great surprise to her grace, who did not expect the young lady. And Strawn had never, as he said more than once, in his born days been so took, for it was Miss Julia returned from the dead, so it was. "Fainted right off, I did," he said, "and it's a wonder her grace didn't die of the shock of it."

Hibbert found his moments of leisure were beginning to fill with doubts. But there was work to do, and he had not the time for speculation. It would all come out in the end.

Although the honored guests were not due to arrive for several days, Lord and Lady Playre—Miss Caroline that was—came up early from London. To help, she told Hibbert.

"While I know that you have everything under control, Hibbert—as you always do—yet we must make sure nothing is left undone for Miss Mortimer and her parents. Nothing that could be criticized, you understand." With a twist of her lips, she added wryly, "My brother's honor is involved."

As indeed it was, to his downfall, Caroline thought. He had agreed to their parents' arrangements for his marriage, and he would not go back on his word. She eyed Hibbert, wondering whether to take him into her confidence, and at last decided against it. Perhaps later, when some marvelous plan might leap into her head, she might command the butler's assistance in order to save Justin from a disastrous match.

"The honor of the house is involved," Hibbert amended. "We shall have everything in readiness, my lady."

After he had left, Caroline was left alone with her thoughts. Her maid, Monk, was busily unpacking her trunks and setting aside gowns to take downstairs for pressing. Gervase was closeted in the library with Justin, and in any event he was prone to tell her she had little reason to doubt Justin's ability to manage his own affairs.

"Besides," Gervase had pointed out accurately, "he will not welcome any interference, and in truth I have noticed that opposition simply makes him more stubborn than before, if that is possible."

So Caroline was forced to keep her own counsel and turn a blind eye to her brother's destruction. Anilee was not a vicious woman, she had to admit, but she was far from intelligent and seemed much more interested in gowns and parties than in Justin.

Lady Playre had a glimpse of her brother's prospects: years of unhappy attempts to make the marriage work. The birth of an heir, or possibly two just to ensure the inheritance, and then long years of loneliness and separation. And Justin didn't even have the excuse of being in love with the woman.

She had seen, moreover, the odd look in Justin's eyes when he watched Pommy Fiske. She had never known him to take trouble over any young female as he had with Pommy. Imagine Justin traveling hastily out of London to overtake the stage and remove the girl from it. The brother she thought she knew was behaving in a totally unpredictable fashion. Love? Perhaps, but it was too soon to be sure. Even so, he would not alter his agreement with Anilee, or more accurately, with Anilee's parents.

Men and their honor!

However, there was one person with whom Caroline knew she could share her misgivings. The day after her arrival at Lisle Court, she borrowed her brother's curricle and drove to Edgecumbe Manor.

Her welcome was all she could have wished for.

"Or did you come to see Pommy?" the duchess inquired. "I know of your kindness in taking her in. She speaks of little else. I'm sorry she is not here at the moment, for the Vivyans have taken her off for the day. She is really a charmer, you know."

"Yes, and why that cousin of hers drummed it into her head that she was too *gauche* to go about in London, I cannot imagine."

"Well, she has lost the battle," the duchess said. "I shall bring Pommy into society myself, this autumn. I have not told her yet, of course."

"Won't Sir Arthur object?"

The duchess's face wrinkled in glee. "He cannot. I have written him, as is my duty," she said piously, "but he's gone to one of those Greek islands he is so fond of and won't be back in England until too late."

Caroline laughed. "I should have known you would know just how to go on. But I should warn you, there is some stir in London about the matter."

"About which matter? Sir Arthur's shameful abandonment of his daughter, or—"

"Not Sir Arthur. Young Frederick Watters is the talk of the town. Has he appeared at your door?"

"Why should he? Oh, I recall some nonsense about his betrothal to Pommy. In truth, I understood from Justin that I might expect to find Bow Street Runners skulking in the shrubbery at the least or even at my door." Lowering her voice so that Strawn should not overhear, she added, "I even ordered Asbury to send up a couple of strong farm workers to stay close for a few days—you know, to help Strawn repel boarders, so to speak."

"How clever of you!"

"But, alas, there was nothing to it. No runners, no

betrothal in all likelihood. Pommy never saw the notice. I think the whole arrangement was playacting to frighten the child into compliance, and I shall not readily forgive that.''

''Ah, but there is something to it. The announcement was in fact in the *Gazette* the very morning Watters took her from my house.''

''But the fool lost her before he got home. At least, that is the tale I was told.''

''That is accurate, as far as it goes. The accident that allowed Pommy to escape from the coach—a closed coach, mind you—gave rise to some inquiries. Mr. Watters was questioned, quite severely I believe, and especially about the identity of the passenger. The woman he was transporting, so they accused him, for immoral purposes.''

''Good God! Don't they have anything better to do than to interfere with a gentleman's pleasure?''

''But they were talking about Pommy. No gentleman's light-skirt.''

''Ah, but they didn't know that, did they? He didn't tell them who she was, did he?''

''I understand not. But since many people knew that Pommy was staying with Lady Derwent, and expected that she would be introduced into society shortly, the gossip mills are diligent, with much material to work with. You see, Pommy has vanished and Lady Derwent tells the most foolish stories to account for her absence. Also, Frederick Watters has disappeared as well. It is thought that the pair has eloped.''

After a thoughtful moment, the duchess nodded to herself. ''Very well. I know how to scotch that rumor. A short note, I think, to Sally Jersey will serve.''

''But what if Mr. Watters comes here? Strawn cannot be much protection for you, even with the farm workers at hand. They cannot be with you always.''

"Don't worry, my dear. That entire Fiske family has the courage of a limpet."

Caroline thought, Timid or not, limpets can be troublesome. But she had warned her grace and there was nothing more she could do. Besides, she had on her mind a subject more important than a dozen Mr. Watters.

To her surprise, the duchess brought up the question. "What are you doing about Justin?"

"What do you mean?"

"I mean the man's hag-ridden. If ever I saw a wretched man, he is it. What is it, that Mortimer woman?"

"He is so miserable," exclaimed Caroline, near to tears. "He's going to marry her, he says, simply because my father thought the Mortimer lands in Hampshire would round out his own estate. I should think the Harcourts had land enough. Certainly they haven't missed the manors that were settled on me when I married."

"And your father made the arrangements?"

"Justin was abroad at the time, sowing wild oats, my father said. Papa thought it best that Justin be prevented from making a terrible mistake in some foreign country, and if he were contracted to marry, he would be safe. As though Anilee was not a disaster herself."

The duchess was intrigued. "You throw quite a new light on your brother's character. Wild oats? I wish you could have known the late duke, my husband. Now he could have defined wild oats for you!"

"Compared with Gervase," Caroline said, "Justin is the soul of adventure."

Curious, the duchess wondered, "Didn't your brother want to choose his own wife?" Perhaps he was not the proper match for Pommy, after all.

"He didn't care then whom he married. He's told me since that he thought it was unlikely that he would ever come back to England, for he expected daily to be brought down by robbers. And now he won't cry off.''

"I suppose he speaks often of honor," the duchess said in a matter-of-fact way. "Men do that. Their ideas of honor and duty are so antiquated. One would think they were living in the days of chain mail and the Crusades.''

"I can't talk to him about it; he won't listen. Besides, Gervase says I must not interfere.''

"Pooh to that," said the duchess. "Justin owes nothing to that flightly miss with the brain of a peahen. No, my dear, I have not met her, but I knew her mother once, and I have friends in London who keep me *au courant* of affairs. Cannot Justin see that the girl is as narrow-spirited as her mother? So many times one need only look at the mother to see what the daughter will be like, and in this instance, the possibility should be sufficient warning to him.''

"He sees it, all right. I do not believe he has spent more than a dozen hours in her company since his return to London, and he never sees her save in company.''

The duchess turned thoughtful. Finally, she said slowly, "Is she taken with Justin, do you think? Or is it his title?''

"I believe it is his title, and his money. The Mortimers appear to be well enough in pocket, but I confess I am uneasy on that head. Those diamonds Lady Mortimer wears are certainly paste.''

The duchess nodded sagely. "Land-poor, I think is the term for a situation in which there is no cash but acres and acres that eat up all the income and more. The duke's family has always been beforehand with the world. But if the Mortimer's are hard pressed, then . . .'' Her voice trailed off. Caroline eyed her godmother with high expectations. Something must be done to save Justin from himself. Since she had had no success with him, her only hope was now sitting opposite her, those deep-blue eyes closed in thought. What kind of miracle was possible?

"It will require a miracle," the duchess said abruptly, "and there's not much time for that. You think title and money are the charm? Just so. If Anilee could be brought to have doubts about one or the other . . ."

Caroline giggled. "I hope you do not mean to find a long-lost oldest son of my grandfather's? He was a shocking loose screw, as I believe, but I never heard of anything really bad. And an illegitimate son would not serve."

"Your grandfather," said the duchess, appearing to be morally indignant, "was not quite nice, but he did have a high regard for the family. I knew him well." She glanced at Caroline, whose eyebrows had ascended almost into her hair. "Not that well," she added.

"You haven't thought of anything," Caroline concluded mournfully. "I did think that Pommy might have caught his attention. I even fancied that he was more than a little interested in her. But he tells me nothing."

"I could not endorse a match with your brother until Pommy's father comes home," the duchess said untruthfully. She lifted her hands in a graceful gesture of resignation. "We are dealing with your brother's future in as autocratic a manner as ever your father did. And he must certainly be kept in ignorance, particularly if we are unsuccessful in preventing his marriage. But don't fret, my dear. Something may come up. In the meantime, when does the happy bride arrive? Will there be entertainment?"

The conversation then slipped into unexceptional channels, dealing with balls and dinners and excursions into the countryside. "And of course you and Pommy will come to everything."

"I shall be most pleased. Pommy must have a ball gown

or two, and I am sure my own gowns are hopelessly dated. Pray let me know as soon as your guests arrive. I must call on them before we meet at any formal dinner.''

"Of course, ma'am. And can you think of something, some scheme? I know you were famous for your intrigues— my mother told me so.''

"I used to be, child. But now, well, who knows?''

13

Pommy had, even before she met the principal guests at Lisle Court, had a sufficiency of weddings.

The servants at Edgecumbe Manor, so Bess, Pommy's maid, told her, spoke of little else but the beauty of the intended bride: her golden curls; her gowns, which were sure to be in the height of London fashion. Bess even sought to try her hand at dressing Pommy's mahogany hair in the same style as Miss Mortimer's. "A bunch of ringlets over the forehead, so," Bess explained.

"You haven't even seen Miss Mortimer," exclaimed Pommy. "The Mortimers have not arrived yet. How could you possibly know how she does her hair?"

Bess seemed bewildered by the question. News in the country traveled in the simplest fashion. Lady Playre's maid, Monk, had seen Miss Mortimer many times in London. When Monk was conveyed in the Playre entourage to Lisle Court, she chose to establish her clear superiority over the court servants by furnishing them with elaborate, exaggerated, details about the lady who was expected to be their mistress. The Lisle Court servants transmitted all they learned to their friends at the manor, and Bess could almost believe she had seen with her own eyes the magnificent Miss Mortimer, who had yet to arrive at Lisle Court.

Bess tried to explain. "Lady Playre's maid—"

"Enough of this," Pommy interrupted, out of sorts. "Tie my hair back in a ribbon. That will have to do."

Sulking, Bess did as she was bid. Miss Pommy was ordinarily the most amiable of mistresses, but these last few days she had been difficult to please.

Pommy knew she had hurt Bess's feelings. It seemed, however, as though the entire world was gathering in congratulatory mood around the lovely lady and the handsome bridegroom at Lisle Court. Even Pommy's day with the Vivyans had been all too full of gossip and speculation.

Miss Simpson, waiting for Pommy now in the sewing room, could be depended upon to make extensive remarks upon the gowns fresh from London, brought by Lady Playre. As is usual with experts on any subject, her vision was narrowed to include only flounces and drapings, bodices and chemisettes and sleeves.

Pommy had seen Caroline only twice since she had arrived. Lady Playre had far too much to do in connection with her brother's expected guests, and of course it was totally unheard-of for Pommy to ride to Lisle Court in search of her only friend. For all Pommy knew, she thought wistfully, Lady Playre could be dressed these days in wimple and farthingale like Queen Elizabeth.

The ball gown was ready for its final fitting, and Miss Simpson gathered the material together and dropped it deftly over Pommy's head. The duchess had climbed to the sewing room to give her final approval.

Kneeling, Miss Simpson tugged this way and that, very gently, until she was at last satisfied. "It hangs better than than I expected," she explained to the duchess. "Urling's net is so difficult to work with."

"Pommy, what do you think?"

The glass was adjusted so she could see herself from curls to slippers. The Urling's net, a new machine-made lace in delicate green, was draped cunningly over a white satin slip, gored to fall in gentle folds from the high waist. For a moment, Pommy caught her breath. She scarcely recognized herself. The gathered green net gave an impression of sea foam rising up around her, and deepened the copper color of her hair.

"It's beautiful," breathed Pommy.

"So it is, and so are you, child. You've been a good girl to stand still for all these dress fittings. Now run along and get some fresh air."

Pommy and Star left the stable yard behind and headed for her favorite ride. Just as Asbury had shown her that first day, she walked Star past the outbuildings and headed for the wall that protected Edgecumbe lands from the public road that paralleled it. The air was heavy this morning, and she was certain a storm was brewing. She could probably make the circuit of the estate and get back to the stables before the rain came.

She had gained the trust of the head groom, and although he did not like to let her ride alone, he knew she rode like the wind, Star was well-mannered, and Pommy rarely strayed from the duchess's lands.

She touched Star's flank, and the mare broke into a trot. Great trees overhung the wall, and the shade beneath them was deep. She was lost in her thoughts and never glanced over the wall. She did not see the watching figure in the road.

The figure in the road was vastly uncomfortable. His London coat was far too warm for the country, he had discovered, and his boots pinched his feet.

Frederick Watters had learned, this past fortnight, that whatever troubles he had in the past paled beside those that

now threatened him. Never one to be beforehand with the
world, he had always relied on his mother to pull his
chestnuts out of the fire. When he lost heavily at the
Newmarket races, his mother had borrowed from his stepfather to cover his debts. When his tab at Watier's had
reached a disastrous sum, which prevented him from gaming
there, again, from somewhere, his mother provided the blunt.
When his stepfather died and his mother learned that her
second husband's debts had eaten his substance, Frederick
could not at the start comprehend that his circumstances were
now altered significantly.

When one's luck goes, he discovered, it goes completely
and immediately. The cards, in his opinion, began to play
him false, and his long run of ill fortune intensified. However, it did not occur to him to cease gambling, for he knew
nothing else to do. He was soon under the hatches, and certain ugly characters entered his life, voicing equally ugly
threats.

Frederick had not wished to marry. Indeed, he considered
that he was not the marrying sort. But it soon developed,
directly after his Cousin Pommy had come to stay with his
mother, that marriage was a fate he must consider.

"Pommy's fortune," his mother told him frequently,
"should stay in the family. I do not hesitate to tell you that
I cannot pay your debts anymore. And I do not wish to see
bailiffs at my door. Best marry Pommy. The marriage will
save both of us."

"She scarcely knows I'm alive. She will refuse me, I know
it."

"Nonsense. She'll do what I tell her to do. Give up your
rooms and return to this house, and I warrant you she will
be glad of your offer." If she did not bring the girl into
society, she would have no other offers, thought Lady

Derwent, and I would think myself a ninny indeed if I could not bring her around.

So Frederick believed that his troubles would be blown away. He moved into his mother's rented house, cutting his expenses and increasing his comfort. Indeed, for a few days all went well. His creditors, being informed in advance of the betrothal, agreed to await the event. Then Miss Fiske vanished from London, and with her, Frederick's expectations. No matter what the outcome of her flight, it was clear that she was determined not to marry her cousin. It was entirely possible, as well, that if she were forced to do so, someone of her family might tie up the money so that young Watters could not touch it.

Besides the reappearance in his life of certain importunate creditors, coming close upon the heels of his fiancée's defection, Frederick found that he was the butt of jokes among his friends. No man likes his bride to advertise to the world that she cannot abide him.

So Frederick made a decision. He would go after Pommy and bring her back. She was betrothed to him, and his intentions were honorable. Who could take exception to that?

Lady Derwent believed that Pommy must have gone to her grandmother's, since there was no other logical place. Pommy's own home, Beechknoll, had been closed while Sir Arthur was abroad. With his mother's directions in hand, Frederick eventually arrived in Middlesex.

The duchess had a formidable reputation, and Frederick was not brave enough to drive up to the front entrance and demand to see his fiancée. It was more than possible he would be told she was not there, whether she had taken refuge at the manor or not. It was much better to make sure of his facts first.

Thus it was that Frederick was in the road outside the

manor when Pommy rode by, unheeding, on the other side of the brick wall. When he heard hoofbeats approaching, he stood up in the curricle, the better to see. And he was in luck. The rider was Pommy. He watched her as far as he could see her. The brick wall extended beyond a rise in the road. How could he get to her? He could now go directly to the front door of the house and demand to see her. But doing so required a brand of courage he did not have. But if he could talk to her . . .

Through trial and error and a kind of fuzzy reasoning, he came to the conclusion that there must be a way into the estate called Edgecumbe Manor other than the neat graveled entrance drive. At length, he found the wagon road that ran, although he did not know it, between Edgecumbe Manor and Lisle Court. His search had taken some time, and he feared that she had returned to the house while he was otherwise engaged.

Nonetheless, he opened the gates and pulled them wide enough for the curricle. He had no intention of walking any distance in those boots. He climbed back into the curricle and set off down the wagon road.

Far down the road he saw someone coming his way, a horse and rider, he thought. Squinting his eyes the better to see, he still could not be sure the rider was Pommy. Suppose, though, it were not Pommy? He must be trespassing and he had no wish to be thrown off the premises in disgrace. Quickly he drove into some shrubbery along the road and tied his horse out of sight. He planned to remain in hiding until he knew who the approaching rider was.

The storm was coming, Pommy observed, and faster than she at first expected. Lightning streaked jaggedly in the dark clouds.

It was time to make for shelter. She cut short her ride a

few fields short of the road along the river and set Star into a canter toward home. The wind ahead of the rain came in strong little gusts, and Star responded nervously, shaking her head and snorting.

Pommy approached the barn where Asbury had told her she could find shelter in case of storm. She might just make the stables, but she and the mare would be soaked, and she liked the lightning as little as Star did. She reined in. It was fortunate for her that she did.

Frederick, peering down the road from behind a tree, recognized Pommy. Who could mistake that red hair? He started out into the road to stop her.

Unintentionally, he scuffed upon some dry leaves, and the wind lifted them, sending them directly in front of the mare. Star took instant exception to the leaves. Adding them to the other grievances on her mind, she reared up, front hooves off the ground, and squealed, a piercing cry of fright and indignation.

Pommy needed all her skill to hold Star. In several minutes she had her under control, but it was out of the question now to try to get to the stables before the rain came. Already thunder rolled near at hand.

At that moment, she became aware of Frederick. "You complete idiot," she said with scalding indignation. "You could have got me killed with that kind of stupid behavior. Don't you know—" She stopped as a new thought struck her. "Or was that your intention? To get me killed? I suppose you are angry with me, but this seems a little beyond everything. Frederick, why are you here?"

"I didn't mean to frighten your mare. But, by Jove, that was something to see. I vow I never saw a female handle a horse—"

"Frederick!"

"I only want to talk to you," he said.

"What about? We have nothing to say."

Frederick felt at a great disadvantage. Not of superior height to begin with, he was forced now to address Pommy towering above him. "I can't talk to you like this," he said plaintively. "Do get down."

Pommy was of two minds. She really had nothing to say to Frederick, save to suggest strongly he return at once to London. But beyond that she did not wish him to come to the house. Her grandmother should not be troubled with this intruder, for that was what he was at Edgecumbe Manor, and if she could send him away now, the duchess would be none the wiser.

Even more urgent than either of these reasons, she must get both herself and her mare under cover. She slid to the ground and led Star toward the barn.

Frederick followed. To detain her, he put his hand on her shoulder.

She whirled to face him, her eyes blazing. "Don't touch me again, Frederick."

Frederick realized that things were again going wrong for him. All he wanted was to tell her she must come back to London with him. He had the pathetic trust of all near illiterates in the power of the printed word. A betrothal was published; therefore a betrothal was valid, and she was bound to do what he told her. That was the way life was supposed to be.

"Where are you going? Into that barn? But we must talk—"

Gritting her teeth and refusing to be goaded into quick retorts, she unlatched the barn door and pulled it wide enough to admit Star. She was very near to pulling the door shut in his face, but he forestalled her.

He looked distastefully at his straw-covered boots. Would his man ever be able to restore the shine?

Pommy must be made to see reason. Once she submitted to the idea of marrying him, he could buy a dozen pair of boots.

"You know, Pommy, our betrothal was announced—"

"You can just unannounce it," she said furiously.

"I don't think you understand. We are engaged. Nothing can change that."

She was seized with a forceful recollection of Justin's situation: nothing could change his betrothal either. In that moment her concentration lapsed and her guard fell.

Frederick, realizing he had not so far given an impression of *beau galant* he believed women expected, took her roughly by the shoulders and planted a wet, inexpert kiss on her lips before she could cry out. Had she screamed, it would have made no difference. At that moment the storm broke and heavy rain drummed on the barn roof.

No one could have heard her.

14

Frederick was not possessed of a powerful intellect, but even he could discern that the lady was unwilling.

Nonetheless, he had his rights, he believed. Besides, he was in too deeply to pull back. He still held her by the shoulders, even though his attempted kiss slid from her lips to her cheek as she turned her head abruptly. His mouth was suddenly and distastefully full of hair.

Pommy realized then that she had seriously underestimated this man. He as in the grip of emotional currents that ran deeper than she guessed. Perhaps he did want to marry her for herself and not for her wealth. As long as only his reason, such as it was, was involved, she could fend him off by her wits. But this was a new Frederick, and alarm stirred in her.

Feeling his grasp easing on her, she placed both hands flat on his waistcoat and shoved him away with all her strength. The best defense . . .

"How dare you, Frederick!" She wiped the wetness from her cheek with the back of her hand. "Have you taken leave of your senses? I've told you before. Do not touch me again, ever! Try to remember I'm not one of your upstairs maids, to be treated so."

"You're the one who's up in the boughs. A little kiss,

what's that to a betrothed couple? Pommy, you've got to remember your duty to your father." He considered a moment and added, "And to me."

"You know, Frederick, no amount of talking can change my mind. Listen carefully: I—shall—not—marry—you."

She wished heartily that this afternoon were done with and she were back in the lovely cream-and-green sitting room that had been her mother's, herself toweled dry, and Frederick only a bad memory.

He was not a memory. Standing a few feet away from her, he was very real. He cocked his head, listening. For the first time, he seemed to be aware of the rain drumming on the roof of the barn. The sound was muffled by the thatch, but it was obvious that the clouds had opened and sent down a downpour of no mean proportions.

He glanced at Pommy wearily, and what he saw was not reassuring. She had backed up against the hayloft wall and watched him with unfriendly eyes. It was time, he decided, to change tactics.

"I'll get my rig under cover," he informed her, "and we'll talk about this. You might as well give in at the start, my girl, for there is no way out of it."

"There's no room in here for your rig."

He looked about at the empty barn. Star was tethered at the far end, and since it was summer, most of the tools usually stored here were in use in the fields.

"There's plenty of room," he protested.

He went to the door and opened it slightly. The rain was falling heavily. He was in no way eager to get out into the storm. He turned to look at Pommy, and the decision to leave his horse and curricle to brave the storm where they were was made at once. He knew as clearly as if she had told him that the minute he was outside, the door would be barred against his return.

Besides, his eyes were accustomed now to the dim interior of the building. Pommy had been lightly dressed for the heat of the day, and her shirt clung to her alluring body. He saw clearly the outline of her small breasts, and his hands itched. He swallowed.

"There's plenty of room in the barn," he repeated hoarsely.

"Get out, Frederick." Her voice was calm enough, but within she trembled.

"No." He closed the barn door and complained, "It never rains like this in London."

Since Pommy had a clear recollection of a recent storm in London, quite as severe as this one, she gave his complaint the attention it deserved.

"Nonsense," she said crisply. "Frederick, why don't you go back to London? You know I shall never marry you."

"Your father wishes it."

"But I do not," she pointed out. "My grandmother will keep me until I am of age, and even if he cared what happens to me, my father cannot make me wed anyone. Especially you."

Nothing was going right for him, Frederick reflected, nor had it since he could remember. His debts were enormous. His luck was out. His last chance at financial salvation now stood before him a few feet away, and was proving exceptionally slippery. Life was proving to be very unfair to him.

Somehow there must be a way to get Pommy's fortune for his own. If he could perhaps compromise her . . . But he had no very clear way of how to go about it. Besides, if his eyes did not fail him, there was a dangerous weapon leaning against the wall too close to Pommy's hand to ignore. He did not know what the five-tined fork was called, but he did not wish for closer acquaintance.

He was moved to waspish speech. "Even your grandmother cannot find a husband for a hoydenish miss like you.''

Pommy had heard such a remark in various forms during her entire sojourn in Berkeley Square. She had believed it, for Cousin Lydia was familiar with the ways of society. But since she had been told sufficiently by her grandmother that there was no fault to find with her manners, she could not be wounded quite as deeply as Frederick intended.

''Then,'' she said calmly, ''I shall not marry.''

''Look at you,'' he said, still attacking and moving forward as he did so, ''riding out without even a groom as escort, I see. Well, as disgraceful as your behavior is, you'll likely marry a groom.''

Frederick did not believe what he was saying. It was of course true that Pommy was not in Hyde Park but on her grandmother's estate, and she did not ride out on the road dressed in such a way, and unescorted as well.

But he had heard his mother's constant corrections of the girl. If they worked for his mother, then possibly he could use the same battering words for his own purpose. But if words were futile, then action must succeed.

He came at her too quickly for her to evade him. The fork was out of reach by the time she realized what he was about. He reached to take rough hold of her shoulders . . .

Her instinct promptly served her. She balled her fist and with all her force drove it into her adversary's nose. She watched him stagger back as far as the door. She was satisfied, but not overly surprised. After all, this was the way one protected oneself against a bullock in the pen.

''Dab you! By dose is bleedig.''

''I told you not to touch me again,'' she said shakily. She leaned against the wall, for her knees seemed without any warning to be made of water, all of a sudden.

''Help me, Pommy. Help me.''

''If I got close enough to help you,'' she pointed out,

"you'll simply try again. Your nose will stop bleeding in a few moments. Try for a little patience."

She was commendably calm on the surface, but within she had no more substance than a blancmange. She longed for the rain to stop so that her foolish self-styled suitor might take his bloody nose and leave, and at the same time she wished the rain to keep her in the barn long enough to exercise sufficient control over her shaking body to mount Star so that she could return to the house.

Star whinnied sharply and stamped a hoof. Was it the small amount of blood that troubled her? Frederick would have to leave, that was certain.

But it was not the smell of blood that troubled the mare. The barn door behind Frederick opened abruptly and a haughty sorrel stallion stood in the doorway. While Star's attention focused on the equine newcomer, Pommy cried out in relief at the gentleman on the ground, holding the reins in one hand.

"Justin!"

Frederick turned awkwardly. He had found a handkerchief somewhere in his clothing and now held it to his nose. "Rutledge," he said in a muffled tone.

"Watters?" Justin said in surprise. "What are you doing here?"

"Tryig to stob this dosebleed," Frederick answered. "She tapped by claret, the she-devil."

Even drenched to the skin as he was, his dark hair plastered to his head, and his jacket running streams of water onto the floor, Justin was quite the most heaven-sent object Pommy had ever beheld.

Coolly, Justin led his mount inside. Glancing at Star at the far end of the barn, he said, "Do you know, I think I will tether Bandit outside. The rain is easing."

When he returned to the barn, moments later, he believed

he had a better grasp of the situation. He surveyed Frederick Watters in an openly disapproving manner. "I wonder that you allow yourself to be seen in such disarray before a gently bred female."

Frederick, all but dancing in frustration, shouted, "She did this to me. Some gently bred female! I swear she could hold her own at Jackson's."

Justin regarded Pommy with respect. "I admire your marksmanship. How did he get here?"

"He said something about a curricle."

Justin had apparently been caught in the worst of the downpour, for water still ran off his jacket, and his sodden whipcord riding breeches revealed his strong body in detail.

"A curricle," exploded Frederick in tones affected adversely by his bleeding nose. "And I cannot think what it will look like when I get back to it. Covered with leaves, no doubt, and filthy, even if I'm fortunate enough that my horse was not run away with it. She wouldn't let me bring it inside the barn."

Justin was hard-put to maintain a grave expression. The timid maiden he had come across in a dark garden in London was proving to have unseen talents.

"You must admit you have received your deserts, Watters. You are certainly trespassing."

"I adbit dothing." Frederick sniffed tentatively. The bleeding had stopped. He wiped his handkerchief across his jacket and waistcoat, trying with pathetic dignity to clean himself up.

Petulantly, he said, "I never thought a gentleman could act so shabbily! Not even the loan of a handkerchief. I tell you frankly, Rutledge, I need no more of your prosing. I know I'm on her grace's property. Pommy was pleased to order me off, you know. But I have some rights here—"

"None," cried Pommy.

"You're becoming tedious, Watters. The rain has stopped, and so has your nosebleed. I suggest you see to your cattle." So saying, he opened the barn door on dripping trees and a watery ray of sunshine.

With a last baleful look at Pommy, Frederick sidled through the door. But he had one last word for Pommy. "You've not seen the last of me."

"Oh, Frederick, do be sensible. Send the cancellation to the *Gazette*."

Frederick realized that he had dangerously outstayed his welcome. It was time to retreat—not in defeat, for the money was as necessary to him as a breath of life itself, an expression to be taken literally, under the circumstances—and see to the repair of his nose. Broken, undoubtedly, and deucedly uncomfortable to boot. He needed time to make new plans. The first place to start was with a strong brandy at the first inn he could find.

No sooner was Frederick out of Pommy's sight than he was out of her mind. Indeed, she had room in her thoughts for no one but the strong, decidedly seductive man a few feet away at the door. Justin looked out, following Frederick with his eyes, and satisfied that he was indeed gone, he stepped back inside the building and closed the door firmly behind him.

"Well, Pommy . . ."

His breath caught in his throat. She was lovely. Her eyes were enormous in her face, thinner now than when he had first seen her. For a moment, he thought he read a special intimacy in her eyes, but it was gone before he could be sure.

He took a few steps, as though drawn to her against his will. His hot gaze lingered on her, sliding caressingly from crown to toe. Her clothes were dry, but wrinkled and still clinging to her slender body in a most provocative way, and his fingers clenched and unclenched. A wave of terrifying passion swept him and he felt curiously disoriented.

He must, she thought, hear the blood pounding in her head as he came toward her. She felt the kiss in his eyes as though his lips had already taken possession of hers. She understood the queer hunger she saw in his brown eyes, for that same need, to feel again his body pressing against her along the entire length of hers, swept her in wordless demand.

She lifted her hand in an oddly appealing gesture, and the mood was broken. He drew a shuddering breath, and the tenseness slowly drained away from his broad shoulders. When he returned to himself, he sought for ordinary words.

"You mentioned the *Gazette*. His announcement was published, after all?"

"So it seems."

"Then you are officially betrothed."

"As are you."

"Not quite yet," he said. "But within a week, I think."

"I wish you happy."

The expressed sentiment was so at odds with his own thoughts and with the unhappiness he saw in her eyes that he took refuge in anger from the powerful wish to crush her in his arms.

"How did that fool Watters come to be in a barn with you? Don't you know any better than to encourage him?"

Startled at the savagery with which he spoke, she stammered, "Of c-course, I do. It was none of my doing."

"He just arrived from London and immediately closeted himself in an isolated building with you? I find that difficult to accept."

Pommy stiffened. "No one, Lord Rutledge, has asked you to accept anything at all. I take it amiss that a person who does not rule his own life should believe he can rule mine."

"Now what does that outbrust signify? I rule my life . . ." His voice died away. The lie was too much even for him to maintain as truth. "You don't understand."

She flared up at him. "I understand well enough, sir. You are meekly allowing other people to control your life and your happiness."

"I must assume you are speaking of my coming marriage. You would suggest, I suppose, that I follow your example. Thank you, I shall not. You control your life by running away. At least I do not give ground."

"As you feel I do? You have it right. Until I am of age, I have no recourse except flight. And may I point out to you, sir, that at least I am not to wed someone I do not wish to marry."

Astounded at her swift and telling retort, he lost his head. "With my assistance, you must agree. And a good thing for you I arrived just now in timely fashion. You have as little sense as an infant. Riding out without a groom is the most feckless thing. No wonder you had to be rescued. But give this some thought, my dear, I may not always be here to rescue you from your folly. Next time—and if I read Mr. Watters correctly, there will be a next time—you may well find yourself wed before you know it."

He opened the door and stood in the doorway. "And," he said as a farewell, "it will serve you right."

She stood without moving for some little time. She was numb. For a moment she had thought he had some regard for her. She was mistaken. She felt battered by Justin's harsh words, as though he had actually thrown rocks at her. He was cruel, a beast, an unfeeling animal with no more sensitivity than that wall.

And the most lowering thing, she longed even now to throw herself headlong into his strong arms and sob her heart out.

* * *

Justin rode home through back lanes and wagon tracks, and hardly knew where he was. He was in a state of mind unprecedented in his more than twenty years. Anger at Pommy predominated in his turbulent thoughts. The girl was too green for words. Of course, her father was to blame. By now Justin knew that Sir Arthur had kept his daughter immured in his estate in Bedfordshire, and only when it suited his convenience had he given thought to her advancement in society.

How was the girl to get along anyway? The duchess might bring her into society, but in the meantime here was this greedy cousin, licking his chops over his anticipated prize. Justin would willingly take on the chore of protecting Pommy against all danger—not chore, privilege. And at that moment he realized where his thoughts were leading.

Anger was displaced by resentment of his father's plans for him, and by disgust at himself for falling in with those plans until it was too late to extricate himself.

Approaching Lisle Court from the fields, he pulled up behind the stables, his attention caught by the activity in the courtyard. Unseen, he watched while the traveling coach of the Mortimers was brought around from the front of the house. The grooms were unhitching the horses. Justin's future had just arrived, and he felt as unmoved as a stone wall.

Absently handing over his stallion to Jenkins, the head groom, he instructed him to rub the animal down, and headed for the kitchen door of his ancestral home.

Flabbergasted, Jenkins led Bandit away. It was the first time his lordship ever let anyone else groom his horse, but thinking on it, Jenkins decided it was only right that his lordship be that eager to greet the lady he was supposed to be marrying. Well enough, he thought, it will be good to have a lady at Lisle Court again.

Justin, however, had no intention of greeting his intended bride. He was in no mood to be civil, he told himself, to say nothing of cordial welcoming.

He met Hibbert as soon as he entered the house. "There you are, my lord. Lady Playre has been asking for you. Sir Henry and Lady Mortimer and of course Miss Mortimer have arrived."

"Let my sister deal with them," Justin said curtly. "I shall be in my study upstairs."

He left Hibbert as openmouthed as Jenkins had been. That man was not an eager bridegroom, Hibbert decided. Something must have happened to put his lordship off, and he wished he knew what it was.

Justin's study had remained unchanged since his father's time. Justin sat now at a great mahogany desk, surrounded by three walls of his father's choicest reading material. He had yet to take down a book from the shelves. The late Lord Rutledge's tastes ran to books of sermons and antiquarian studies.

It was gradually borne in on him that as his father's preferences in reading were not to rule his life, neither should his father's ideas on other subjects have undue influence. Justin was still at a far distance from abandoning his marriage plans, but his entire happiness was now at stake and he must take thought before acting irrevocably.

He suspected that he was more than halfway in love with that abominable Pommy. This entanglement had crept upon him unaware, and he heartily wished it hadn't. How could he make logical decisions when the innocent appeal in her smoky gray eyes appeared unbidden before him every moment of his day?

At length he became aware that the room was darkening.

He did not know how long he had sat unmoving, contemplating his future. It was twilight, however, and time to pick up his duties as host of the house party.

He still did not know what he intended to do.

15

It was the third day after the arrival at Lisle Court of the guests of honor.

The Mortimers had settled in nicely. Lady Playre was not surprised to detect a furtive tendency on their part to examine furniture when no one was watching, to regard paintings hanging on the walls with an appraiser's eye, and to display a certain regrettable haughtiness in dealing with the Lisle Court servants. One of the kindest things she would do in her life, she judged, was to spare Hibbert and his staff the undeserved burden of Anilee as their mistress.

Busy with her duties as hostess for her brother, Caroline had not been free to drive again to Edgecumbe Manor to visit the duchess. Lady Playre longed to know whether her grace had devised some plan to deal with Anilee Mortimer. She had to confess that her own mind was so filled with tending to the constant details involved in managing a large country-house party that there was no room left to develop any kind of scheme. Perhaps after the coming dinner party inspiration would visit her.

This afternoon, however, the first of the grand entertainments planned for the edification of the Mortimers was to be held. Gaston, Justin's French cook, had for days maintained a reign of terror in his kitchen. It was not every day that he was asked to prepare a lavish dinner to introduce Lord Rutledge's intended bride to the surrounding neighborhood, and he made the most of it.

And Gaston was not alone in anticipation.

At Edgecumbe Manor, Pommy dressed for the dinner. She was in an uncertain frame of mind. If she had had an extensive wardrobe, her gowns would have been donned one after another and discarded in disgust. As it was, the only suitable garment for the event was the nearly finished net gown in sea-foam green. However, even that dress had been on and off more than once, to the growing impatience of Aggie, her grace's maid.

"Best keep it on this time," Aggie advised sourly. "Her grace will be wanting to leave. She's already ordered the carriage." Standing back after arranging one last curl, she added, "You look as good as can be. Stop fussing, miss. It's not becoming for a young lady to think too much of her looks."

Pommy's reluctance to dress was not caused by dissatisfaction with her appearance. She had little vanity, and beyond that, she was sure that Miss Mortimer would be the center of all eyes. Her restlessness was caused quite simply by her wish not to see Justin again. She dreaded meeting his fierce glare, to be accused again of running away and of various examples of culpable behavior. In the barn that day, his anger had been savage and above all unjustified, and she had had quite enough of that. But it would be worse, she thought, if he were to look at her with cool indifference, as might well be the case, with Anilee at his side.

"You're as ready as ever will be, Miss Pommy," Aggie said crossly. "I'll fasten your pearls for you. I remember your mother wearing them to her first party. Well, what's past is past. Then it's off to the party. I don't understand you, miss, and that's a fact. A pretty girl like you and not wanting to go to a party? Beyond me.''

"I'm too brown, Aggie.''

"Too much sun, that's true. But the green does look nice. Her grace has style, that's what she's got. Best learn from her, Miss Pommy. You can't go wrong.''

Can't go wrong? I wish you could persuade Lord Rutledge of that, Pommy thought. Not for the first time in the last few days she had regretted leaving Beechknoll, even though there had been no choice. Even more she regretted running away at the wrong moment from Cousin Lydia's house, for look what that had led to. If she had postponed her departure for only a day until the storm had passed through, she would have been wiser. And she had nearly done so.

Ruefully she thought, I'd run away again—this time I suppose from Justin—if there were someplace to run to.

There was a tap at the door and the duchess entered.

Pommy breathed, "Oh, my.''

The duchess was indeed a spectacle to see. She wore a gown of silk crepe the color of ashes of roses, over a satin slip of the same color, and ornamented at the hem with a wide band of deep-rose shells of satin.

For jewels, she wore the famous rope of splendid emeralds. It was Pommy's first sight of her mother's dowry, supposed to have been turned over to Sir Arthur upon his marriage to Julia. The duchess, disliking Sir Arthur in the extreme, had refused to let the jewels go. "I shall give them to my eldest granddaughter,'' she had said grandly at the time. At this moment her eldest and only granddaughter stood before her. The duchess had long since added a silent postscript to her statement—"when I have done with them.''

The duchess examined her granddaughter critically. At last she pronounced her to be acceptable. "You look very nice indeed," she said. "That green looks beautiful with your hair." After a moment, she spoke in an altered voice. "You look so like your mother, it quite makes me faint. But you have a sweetness that she did not have."

And a vulnerability, she added silently, and I shall not rest until you are safely wed, and not to that cawker who appeared a few hours since.

She changed the subject. "My dear, I have the most startling news. That young man from London arrived this afternoon. I quite see why you removed yourself from his vicinity. A most unpleasant, disreputable-appearing person. Even his mother would be ashamed of him."

"You mean Frederick?" cried Pommy, dismayed. "What did he want? You should have sent for me, ma'am. I am sorry you had to meet him."

"I vow I could hardly understand him. Something seemed to have happened to his face, and he spoke quite dreadfully through his nose. A curricle accident, I should imagine. You were resting and I could handle the situation quite well."

"He went away? Without making trouble?"

"Well, of course he made trouble. But he was easily removed. Strawn and the men from the stables were quite a sufficient force. For myself, I think the man is mad."

"He will not give up," Pommy said, resigned. "He thinks we are betrothed. Of course, officially we are."

"Nothing of the sort. I do not recognize anything that Derwent woman does. Never mind, my dear. He can do you no harm. I shall see to that. Come now, the carriage is waiting and Doughty doesn't like his cattle to stand."

Once on the road to Lisle Court, the duchess relaxed. Her granddaughter was in excellent looks, and she herself reveled in the excitement of dressing lavishly and going into society. She had led much too retired a life, she thought, and her gratitude toward her granddaughter for providing the necessity of changing her ways was deep.

She had given thought to her conversation with Lady Playre. They agreed that Justin's marriage must be stopped. There was little hope that Justin could be brought to cry off, since like all men he clung to some foolish idea that a promise made was a promise kept. Pooh to that!

But she must think of something, and at the moment her mind was unnervingly blank.

At about the same hour that the carriage from Edgecumbe Manor was traveling to Lisle Court, upstairs in that building the residents were making ready for the dinner party.

In a small bedroom next to the suite placed at the disposal of her parents, Anilee Mortimer sat before her dressing table. Her thoughts, for once, were not focused on the truly beautiful face she saw in the mirror.

Nor was she thinking, as one might suppose, of the handsome and wealthy man who was about to claim her as his bride. If the announcement were not made at the dinner that afternoon, Anilee for one would be greatly surprised.

Her thoughts at this moment, however, did not dwell on the luxurious future in store for her, but instead concentrated lovingly on an even handsomer and much more dashing gentleman, Captain Alexander Wolver, who had unaccountably appeared at Lisle Court that morning.

Anilee was more than half in love with Alexander. She had regrettably been forced to terminate her acquaintance in view of her approaching marriage. He had been safe enough as an occasional escort, since her marriage arrangements were unchangeable. However, Lord Rutledge failed miserably in the role of devoted suitor, and a girl had to have an escort, did she not?

Captain Wolver had not been turned away from Lisle

Court. Anilee did not question his presence. Just now she reflected upon broad shoulders, a wickedly beguiling smile, a voice made expressly to melt the bones of impressionable young ladies, and she smiled.

After an heir was produced for Lord Rutledge, she mused dreamily, Alexander might provide sufficient diversion to make her marriage palatable. Or even before that happy event, if it were long in coming.

Her dreams were abruptly shattered when, without knocking, her mother swept into the room. Her grim expression boded no good for her daughter. Lady Mortimer wore a loose dressing gown of gray flannel over her underclothes.

"Mama," Anilee squeaked. "You're not dressed yet? You'll be late for dinner."

"Don't speak to me about dinner. Tell me one thing, missy, did you send for that mountebank?"

"W-who?"

"The captain, that's who. Captain Whatever-his-name-is, Wolver! Did you?"

"Of course not, Mama. I know better than that."

"Then why is he here?"

"I don't know, Mama. Truly, I don't."

"Then how did he get here? How did he even know where to find us? He was forbidden our house in London, and now he shows up here in this forsaken place in Middlesex. Someone must have informed him."

Anilee could not refrain from smiling. It was so like Alexander, she thought. Knowing he was so disliked by her parents that he was not allowed to see her, he came up here to Lisle Court—just like his devil-may-care ways to defy convention, not to care what anyone thought of him.

"I mistrust that smile, young lady," her mother said forbiddingly. "You will not be so lighthearted when Rutledge cries off."

"Oh, no, Mama, he couldn't!" Anilee was horrified. "I did not tell Captain Wolver anything. I have not seen him for a month."

Her denial rang true in her mother's ears, and Lady Mortimer's features relaxed. "That's my girl. I knew you'd see what is best for you. Wolver's not got a feather to fly with, and I will not let you throw yourself away on him."

Captain Wolver had not entertained, at least for long, the idea of marriage to Miss Mortimer. He lived well beyond his income, and his goal was to find an adoring female with a large fortune or the prospects of inheriting well and settling down.

But in the meantime, it gave him some amusement to flirt successfully with a lady on the verge of betrothal to someone else, and more particularly as an uninvited guest.

Lady Mortimer spoke earnestly. "Anilee, I do not wish you to undergo privation as I have done these years. Scrimping every day, striving to put up a good front so that you may marry well. The worst of all was while your father arranged with old Lord Rutledge for your marriage. To pretend to that old man that we were well in pocket! I shudder to remember the schemes I was forced to, the lies . . . Well, it worked out well. I will not allow you to throw it all away."

Anilee had a strong streak of self-preservation. She had no intention of allowing Lord Rutledge—or rather his title and his fortune—to get away. But she saw no need for martyrdom either, and she enjoyed the captain's flirtatious company. She also saw no need to confide her thoughts to her mother.

"Mama, don't be afraid. I know exactly how to treat Captain Wolver. He is merely a flirt, you know, and he'll soon leave. But, after all, if Lord Rutledge does not wish him here, why did he not send him away?"

* * *

Justin had no intention of sending Wolver away. In truth, he was only marginally aware of the man's presence. At this moment, Lord Rutledge sat in his study, hands folded on the top of the mahogany desk, looking at nothing tangible in the room. He had spent a substantial amount of time in this way during the last three days, looking at his future, as it were, and finding therein no pleasure.

It had been three days since his encounter in the barn with Miss Melpomene Fiske, and try as he would, he could not forget the words they had exchanged—words designed, on his part at least, to wound. Why should it be so? Why did he want to hurt her? He told himself, honest for once, that his anger was the only choice he had, other than taking her forcefully in his arms and kissing her with determination. He was not free to do this, nor did he know whether he ever would be.

Never before had he been swept by such a passion as that which impelled him in her direction in the barn. It was as though his mind slept and only his hunger for the girl existed. He was ordinarily a calm, even remote individual. Now he had a glimpse of what might be—that is, of what might have been. He would never again experience such an emotion—never again, that is, would he feel alive.

He recalled all too clearly the wounded shock in her eyes when he lashed out at her. She should not have been riding out alone, but it was not her fault that Watters was no gentleman. After all, Pommy was on private land and could not be expected to come across a London ne'er-do-well on a wagon road in Middlesex.

Were he to follow his inclination, at this moment he would be on his way to Greece to persuade Sir Arthur that he himself was a better match for Pommy than Lady Derwent's son. He knew what his own father would say: no Harcourt goes back on his word. But it was his father's word that had been given, not his. A moral quibble? Perhaps. But he could not decide to avail himself of the loophole thus provided.

The French clock on the mantel ticked loudly in the silence. The sounds of the household came to him from far away, and he did not heed them.

Pommy would be arriving soon, as well as the other guests for dinner. Could he take her aside and apologize for his behavior the other day? Not with Anilee watching. While he could sustain peals rung over him, he was not willing to put Pommy at Anilee's mercy.

Moreover, his was not the only apology in order. Pommy had scored on him as well. He winced at the recollection of the truths she had hurled at him like lances. "You are meekly allowing other people to control your life," she had said. And while he had accused her of running away from all her troubles, she had capped the whole exchange by the truth: "At least I am not to wed someone I do not wish to marry."

Only Justin Harcourt, he concluded ruefully, was so masterful as to be towed by the nose into a marriage he had no part in making.

Upstairs, in the suite of rooms that had been hers before her marriage, Lady Playre dressed for the dinner that was intended to introduce Anilee Mortimer and her parents to local society. She had no doubt that Justin, using the dinner as a significant occasion, intended to make the announcement of his betrothal this very night.

Lord Playre made yet another turn at the far end of the bedroom and came back toward her.

"Please, Gervase," she begged in a voice indicating patience now exhausted, "do stop pacing the floor. I've already got the headache, and you simply make it worse."

Moving directly to the point that worried him, Gervase

demanded, "How did that rounder have nerve enough to invite himself to a Harcourt family party?"

Caroline sighed. "I wonder whether a few drops of landanum would help?"

Her husband said bluntly, "You'll be facedown in your soup plate if you start dosing yourself. I asked you about that Wolver fellow."

For the simple reason that she had no wish to explain all the machinations and concealments she had been forced to in order that a suggestion be made—merely a suggestion—to Captain Wolver that Anilee pined for his company and would not be displeased were he to arrive at Lisle Court unannounced, Caroline remained silent.

However, Gervase was not inexperienced in the ways of his wife. He regarded her sternly and announced his unwelcome conclusion. "You asked him here."

"I did not invite him. But even had I wished to, I suppose I may ask a guest to the house where I grew up?"

"It is not your house. Did your brother agree to having him here? I cannot believe Justin is so mean-spirited as to invite Wolver's presence while Miss Mortimer's engagement is announced? The world knows that the captain is more than smitten with the girl and only the lack of money keeps them from marrying."

"Of course my brother would not be so spiteful. Even if he cared about Anilee, he would not be so boastful as to score off Captain Wolver."

"I believe you would stop at nothing to break up his marriage. Will you swear to me, madam, that you had nothing to do with Wolver's arrival?"

Madam! When Gervase called her madam, she knew he was serious, and quite likely angry as well. She would not lie to her husband, however, no matter how cavalier her attitude to truth in other directions.

"Gervase, I promise you I did not invite the man."

She held her breath, but he seemed to believe the stark statement, even though it left so many other facets of the Wolver affair unaddressed.

She had thought that the appearance of Wolver might well tempt Anilee to an indiscretion—one, hopefully, of such dimensions that Justin would consult his precious honor and cry off. And such a time as she had had with the scheme, too. The hints dropped in one ear, the careless but informative statements in another quarter—all to the successful end that Captain Wolver believed his Anilee pined for him and had somehow persuaded Lord Rutledge into compliance with her wish to see him, Wolver.

Successful Caroline had been, and this very morning she watched with gratification Anilee's delight at the sight of Captain Wolver advancing toward her across the foyer. To her dismay, however, Justin did not seem to care that a gentleman whose name had been seriously linked with Miss Mortimer's had appeared on the eve of her betrothal to Justin.

Was her dear brother too resigned even to care?

While Gervase seemed to accept her denial, yet she could detect a kind of uncertainty in him. At length he said, "Caroline, I warn you, do not interfere in your brother's affairs. He will not thank you for it. I cannot see why you are so set against Miss Mortimer. After all, you will not be required to see her above once a year."

And that, too often, she considered. "Dear Gervase," she told him, "it is only that I want my brother to be blessed with as happy a marriage as I have."

She had struck the right note. His expression softened and he bestowed a kiss on her bare shoulder. "Well, then, my dear, I cannot scold you for that. But leave Justin alone."

She heard the sound of carriage wheels on the graveled

drive. The guests were beginning to arrive and she must be ready to receive them.

Gervase held the door open for her. As she passed him, he said in a low voice, "Now, mind, Caroline. None of your tricks! Promise me?"

"Of course, dear," she said with a sunny smile.

Thank God, she thought, he did not see my fingers crossed.

16

The dinner party, thought Pommy, was fully as dreadful as she had feared. Justin had greeted her grandmother affably and Pommy herself with a shuttered expression. There was no discerning his thoughts behind his impassive expression, but it was most probable that she would not be pleased if she knew. He had clearly not forgiven her for the accusations of, call it cowardice, that she had hurled at him in the barn three days since.

Moreover, she had every reason to be grateful to him, for she was not sure she could have defended herself against Frederick's next rush, maddened as he was by his injured nose and his bruised sensibilities. It would have been only a matter of moments, she feared, before he returned to the attack. With that barley fork at hand, she might have done him a mischief of huge proportions that she would later regret. Justin had rescued her in time.

She did not know what she ate at dinner. Probably there was a clear soup and several removes. On the other hand, she was acutely aware of Justin at the end of the table, eating little and entering the conversation in a most proper fashion. Several times she glanced up to find him watching her, and she felt her cheeks flush under his scrutiny.

The party, the duchess thought, was a disaster. She did not judge the food adversely, since she held a strong belief that Justin's cook was inferior to her own and she expected merely passable dishes. But there was an unmistakable atmosphere of vivacity and brightness that was as false as her own earlier complimentary greeting to the Mortimers.

Everyone was trying too hard to make the dinner a success. There was one thing on the minds of everyone around the table: the impending announcement by Justin that his marriage to Anilee Mortimer was signed, if not sealed and delivered.

The Mortimers were eating their way steadily through all of Gaston's offerings. That odd military person—Captain Wolver?—seemed entranced by Pommy, and Anilee pouted. It was left to the Vivyans, the rector and his wife, and several other guests to carry on a limping conversation.

Her grace was granted a flash of inspiration that she considered a gift of providence. The Mortimers cleaned their plates with single-minded concentration, she noticed. Her late husband the duke had several relatives whose fortunes were small and who relied on a month or two at Woodburn to ease their expenses. They, she recalled, ate in just such a dedicated fashion. Therefore, it was reasonable to suppose that the parents of Justin's intended bride might not be as full in the pocket as she had assumed.

Money and title—Caroline had spoken of them as the motivating forces behind Anilee's marriage plans. The title was impeccable. But perhaps money?

Imperceptibly, her manner changed. She became at once more regal and more condescending, particularly to Anilee's parents. She knew well the stunning impact of inherited wealth, and she was gratified to find that the old instincts were never lost.

Fingering in an apparently casual manner the simple rope

of unparalleled emeralds, she addressed Lady Mortimer. "I should like you to become acquainted with our little valley while you are visiting here. After all, I expect you will be returning to Lisle Court from time to time."

Justin fixed her grace with a quizzical glance. What was she up to?

Lady Mortimer, pleased at being noticed by the duchess, stammered an incoherent answer. Her husband looked up quickly, fork poised, listening.

"It will be my pleasure," purred the duchess, "to guide you myself, a small afternoon trip for your little family. Suppose we say two days hence? Will that suit?"

"Of course, your grace. We shall be delighted."

"I insist that Miss Mortimer come as well. Since Lisle Court will be her home, she should find the environs most interesting."

Lady Playre was stunned. Her godmother had gone over to the enemy! Taking them around, introducing them to all the villagers and the tenants—under the aegis of the duchess herself. Caroline felt betrayed. She glared at her grace, incensed. The duchess, however, caught her eye and gave her the merest hint of a wink, one no one else noticed. Caroline sighed in relief. The alliance was still in force.

Pommy noticed nothing of the exchanges between her grandmother and the Mortimers. As the dinner approached its end, she hurriedly put down her fork so no one would notice her hand trembling. She did not know how she would react when Justin rose to his feet to make the fateful announcement. Would she burst into tears on the spot, or mercifully, could she control herself until she returned to the manor and her own room? That was too much to hope for. She would be content were she able to reach the carriage before she broke down in sobs.

She did not know precisely why she felt so low in her mind.

She was not jealous; she had no call to be jealous. But she heartily wished the blond beauty, dressed tonight in virginal white, would take a long and hopefully perilous journey. Alone.

All things come eventually to a close, as did Justin's dinner. The dessert plates had not been removed, but it was almost the moment for clearing the table when the ladies would retire to the largest of the three salons and the gentlemen would be left with their bottles of aged port.

If ever an announcement were to be made, now was the proper time. Justin rose to his feet. He nodded dismissal to Hibbert, who departed, but no farther than the other side of the door.

A rustling sound filled the room, of skirts adjusted, of silver set to rest on china, of anticipation. Pommy shivered.

"I wish," Justin began, "formally to welcome you all to Lisle Court. My family . . ." He bowed to his sister, then to his brother-in-law. "My dear neighbors . . ." He bowed to the duchess, but his eyes lingered long on Pommy. "My friends . . ."

Whatever else he would have said went unspoken, then and forever. Into the rapt silence of the dining room came a great knocking, as though a fist pounded on the oak entrance door.

Justin turned, irritated, toward the door into the hall. The door opened at that moment and Hibbert appeared.

"My lord, I regret the interruption—"

"What are you about, Hibbert? What is that racket?"

Hibbert did not answer at once, but turned to look quickly over his shoulder. "Good God, what—"

Caroline recovered first. "Wake Duncan with thy knocking!"

Lady Vivyan said, with a nervous titter, "Who is Duncan?"

There was a turbulence in the foyer. In the doorway to the

dining room appeared a man much the worse for drink. His waistcoat was disheveled and his hair had not seen a comb for some time. If he had a neckcloth, it was not presently visible.

Holding to one arm was a diminutive footman and to the other was a red-faced Hibbert.

Justin recognized his informal caller. He shot a glance at Pommy, noting the horrified expression she wore.

"Well, Watters," Justin said in a calm voice. "What are you doing here? I must point out your manners are more fitting a barn than my house."

"I want my bride. You can't have her, she's mine."

The duchess was of two minds: to faint and divert the company so that the Watters boor could be removed discreetly, or to stay alert and enjoy herself. The latter choice won.

"You are badly foxed," Justin said.

"Just a li'l brandy for my nose," Frederick explained. "And she wouldn't let me in the house." His little bloodshot eyes focused uncertainly on the duchess.

Captain Wolver saw his opportunity. He had been much impressed with the wealth that the duchess wore as casually as though she were at home in her own salon. The emeralds alone, if they were real—and the captain had a trained eye—would set him up in ease for the rest of his life. And the auburn-haired beauty might well be the only heir.

The intruder, so Captain Wolver believed, had inimical intentions toward the duchess. The captain, springing to his feet, exclaimed, "Rutledge, let me take care of this buffoon. I've dealt with his kind often enough."

Justin nodded curtly. "Hibbert, assist Captain Wolver as he requests." He turned back to the table. Facing him were a group of fascinated and astounded people. Probably never in their lives had a dinner party been interrupted in such an exciting fashion. The intrusion had rather the flavor of the alarms and raids of the ancient Scottish clans. It was not by accident that words from *Macbeth* had sprung to Caroline's lips.

"My apologies to you," Justin said. "This interruption has certainly shattered the festive mood of this occasion."

In a short time Wolver returned. "He's off. And I wager he will not return again."

"My thanks," Justin said coolly. "I did not myself wish to soil my hands on him." It was a clear snub, and Wolver flushed angrily. Justin did not appear to notice. "Your grace—"

The duchess rose, catching the eyes of the female diners, and led the ladies from the dining room. There would be no announcement tonight, that was sure. She had not thought she would ever be grateful to that woman's son, but he had successfully diverted Justin from whatever announcement he was about to make.

However, this was only a momentary respite. There was no time to waste before putting her newly hatched plan in motion.

Frederick Watters was bruised in body and in spirit. He had gone to Edgecumbe Manor that morning to talk to Pommy, but he was sent away by a pair of powerful and unfriendly farmers, but not before learning that the residents would be traveling to Lisle Court for dinner.

This afternoon, after soothing the pain of his wounded nose with a brandy and then another one or two, he decided to join the dinner party. Surely no one would object if he spoke to Pommy in company? He no longer knew what he wanted to say to her. It was a simple obsession—to get Pommy to marry him. And when her fortune was his, he could pay enough of his debts to be allowed back into the various gambling houses where he was not welcome now.

Bruised once more in a never-ending series, so it seemed, of violent physical attacks on his person, he came to the conclusion that he would be better off in London.

His skin, once healed, might remain intact in the city, unless, of course, the "collectors" for his creditors were able to find him.

The duchess had already forgotten the letter she had sent with such pleasure to Pommy's father, hard upon the girl's arrival. If she thought of it, she would have imagined the letter in a musty diplomatic bag taking two months by ship and small boat to arrive at a small rocky island somewhere near Asia Minor. But the letter, which had only gone to Rome, had been delivered as soon as it had been extricated from the diplomatic bag at the British embassy.

Sir Arthur Fiske knew the hand that addressed it. With a muffled epithet, he crumpled the missive and threw it into a corner. The only word he wished to hear from his mother-in-law was that she was sending him the famous emeralds.

His disappointment had been searing when he learned that the emeralds—a truly royal set of jewels—were not to be put into his hands. They were part of Julia's dowry, and Julia should have had them. After Julia's death, of course, ownership, but not possession, devolved upon Julia's daughter, and the old witch still kept them in her talons.

He could use the money from their sale or pledge for his underfunded expedition. Since his own money was tied up for Pommy's benefit, it was only fair that she should give the emeralds to him. And so she should, if she had them!

The Greeks or the Ottomans remained belligerent, and Sir Arthur was held up in Rome. Several days after the duchess's letter had come, a servant finally espied it in a dark corner, smoothed it out, and placed it on Sir Arthur's desk.

Having nothing else to do, Sir Arthur opened the letter and

began to read: ". . . would consider a woman as common as Lydia Derwent a suitable chaperone . . . marriage between Melpomene and that feeble Watters boy . . . few remaining wits . . ."

Sir Arthur read thus far with kindling ire. The words were intended to gore, but he never expected otherwise from her grace. It was the last sentence that sent him into the street, roaring. "I am happy to inform you," wrote the duchess, "that she is safely here with me."

Safely! His daughter safely with the duchess? He could not have been more irate had the Vikings taken to pillaging his Bedfordshire acres.

He walked through the streets, alternating in his mind between wishing to throttle the duchess and ringing a great peal over his Cousin Lydia. When at last he was calm enough to consider the facts conveyed in the duchess's letter, several points occurred to him.

He had received letters from Lydia, to which he had, to be honest, paid little attention. His sole interest lay in the excavation he planned on an island where he expected from his studies to find a heretofore-unknown temple to Hera. He had placed his daughter in safety, he thought, and commissioned his cousin to arrange a suitable match for the girl. He would himself of course withhold final approval until he returned to England, but the tedious business of routs, balls, parties, and other courtship customs would be spared him.

Back at his rooms, he rummaged his desk to find Lydia's most recent letter, hoping it might shed light in dark places. Here it was: Frederick was quite taken with Pommy, she wrote. "I should never approve of that fool as a son-in-law," Sir Arthur muttered. But there was more: "Just as well," Lydia informed him, "since she was so badly brought up, she is ineligible for a society marriage."

Sir Arthur should have paid more attention to this letter when it first came. He thought he had done well for his daughter. It was true, he had little to do with her, but someday he would explain to her that she was so much like Julia—her smoky eyes and her gorgeously auburn hair—that he felt the pangs of loss every time he looked at her. No man should be expected to live like that, grieving anew several times a day.

But he had been careful to see that she received an excellent education, and her governesses were of the highest caliber. It occurred to him also that when Pommy was first in London, Lydia had not complained of her upbringing. In fact, quite the opposite.

But his Pommy in the hands of the woman he considered his greatest enemy! That would never do!

He made good speed up the Italian peninsula and the beautiful countryside of France. He fought off the temptations of Paris, endured a wind-driven crossing to Dover, and appeared in Berkeley Square at about the same time that Frederick returned, disgruntled and disfigured, from his sojourn in Middlesex.

Sir Arthur's arrival caused dismay and a little apprehension in Lady Derwent's heart. Unknowingly, she was in agreement with the duchess in believing Sir Arthur to be well out of reach of mail. Although she had told Pommy she had written her father for, and received, permission for Pommy to marry Frederick, she had lied. She had, in fact, scarcely given Arthur any thought at all.

Now here he was on the doorstep, and apparently not in an amiable frame of mind.

His baggage brought in and a room made ready for his stay, Sir Arthur demanded explanation. "Where is Pommy?"

Lydia Derwent considered. Perhaps Arthur did not know where she was. Could they get her back from the duchess in time to avoid unpleasant questions? She looked across her salon to where Frederick slumped in a chair. His poor face was battered and she suspected his nose was broken. There was, obviously, no chance of recovering Pommy if one had to depend upon Frederick.

"I do not like to tell you—"

"Then I'll tell you!" He took the fateful letter from his pocket and shook it, still folded, in her face. "That's where she is. With the dowager Duchess of Woodburn, that's where. And of all the places I want to see her, that is the absolute last one."

"We could not help it, Arthur. She ran away."

"Why? She's never run away in her life before."

"Probably," Lydia said waspishly, "because she always had her own way at Beechknoll."

"And why should she not?" he asked simply. "So. She ran away from you. And went to Middlesex? How did she know where her grandmother lived?"

"Someone told her, and it was not I. I think she said a governess informed her."

Sir Arthur muttered, "That Miss Horne! She was always a busybody. So she went to Middlesex from here. How did she—"

Lydia interrupted. "Oh, no, not from this house. At least the second time. She ran away, but then we got her back and she ran away again from Frederick." Too late she realized she was giving away information she would have been wiser to keep for herself. "She's totally unbiddable," she defended herself. "Unruly as well, and as lost to proper decorum as ever I saw."

"Don't give me that argument, Lydia," Sir Arthur said coolly. "I know she has unexceptionable manners. I had the best governesses for her. I would never give that harpy the duchess the slightest opening for criticism."

"Then you think running away, traveling unescorted around the country, is well-mannered? I vow you have a different notion of what is proper than I do."

Sir Arthur winced, but he returned to the attack. "What made her run? I don't blame her for a moment, for I am persuaded there were good reasons for her to leave." He turned to Frederick. "Speaking of ill-bred brats, what did you do to her?" He stopped short, noticing Frederick's condition for the first time. "What happened to your nose? I suppose you fell afoul of a boxer at Jackson's."

Frederick felt unloved. Not one word of sympathy had he received on behalf of his broken nose, not even from his mother. He spoke as a man bearing a bitter grudge. "Your daughter did this."

Sir Arthur stared at him. "She did what?"

"She punched me and broke my nose, that's what she did."

"Your charming impeccably mannered daughter, Arthur," Lady Derwent pointed out.

Sir Arthur gave a whoop of laughter. "Did she now! I had no idea she was so much like her grandmother. If she produced that beauty of a nose, I'm sure you did something to deserve it." Turning grave, he added, "And I warn you, you will not do it again, or you will regret it even more."

Lydia Derwent saw all her dreams dissipating. She no longer saw a fortune in her hands. That dream of Pommy's marriage to her son fled with Frederick's narration of his experiences in Middlesex. Now even the hope of a competence settled on her by Sir Arthur in recognition of her efforts in bringing Pommy into society no longer existed.

"It's not our fault," she said sullenly. "If she resembles the duchess, then even you can't handle her, Arthur."

"I'll handle her," he said. "I'll have to get my daughter out of her grandmother's hands. But there's no hurry. As long as I'm in London, there's someone I want to see at the museum. Much as I hate to admit it, Pommy's safe with the old woman. For the moment."

17

Safe Pommy might be, but happy she was not.

Justin had not come into her life in the ordinary way. The ritual of courtship was rigorously established. Parents presented their daughters to society in a wealth of parties. The young ladies were on display, as it were, for eligible gentlemen to choose. Parents saw to it that fortune-hunters, gamblers, and other loose screws were kept away. Even before a suitor became serious, his assets, income, and family history were studied by the prospective bride's parents. Only after this investigation, carried on in a matter-of-fact manner, certified that the young man was acceptable was he allowed to be alone with the lady in order to offer for her. Even after a betrothal was announced, the happy pair was not allowed their privacy. Many a bride went to her new husband as though to a stranger.

Pommy, however, realized that the enforced intimacy resulting from their first and very unconventional meeting gave her a more penetrating insight into his personality than anyone else. She wondered whether she were the only person who suspected the depth of his unhappiness.

Her interest in his well-being, she told herself, was simply because he had brought her safely to Edgecumbe Manor. She was in debt to him also for recognizing Frederick as the great nuisance he was and for removing him from her presence. She had no wish . . . She rephrased the thought: she had no expectations of taking Anilee's place in his life. She kept her private wishes at bay.

At least Frederick was gone. It was now two days after the dinner party at Lisle Court, from where he had been removed without dignity, as though he were a common drunk. The thought briefly crossed her mind that Frederick's dignity was dear to him and he might well seek revenge upon the causes of his humiliation.

But there had been no sign of him at Edgecumbe Manor, and servants' gossip, relayed to her by her maid, indicated that he had left the village inn. She believed he must have returned to London, possibly to seek medical help for his broken nose. She regretted injuring him, but on the other hand, he had certainly brought his troubles on himself.

This day was the one appointed by the duchess to regale the Mortimers with a drive through the countryside.

"I suspect that Miss Mortimer is looking forward to this excursion with the same happy anticipation as a visit to the tooth-drawer," said the duchess with a complacent smile. "She has expressed a distaste for the country, and perhaps I can show her what her life as Lady Rutledge will be like."

"But she will not need to live here," objected Pommy. "She will expect a house in London, and I suspect she will never come to Lisle Court except under duress."

Her grace looked sharply at her granddaughter. "Where do you come by that opinion?"

"Because she never sets foot out of doors. Caroline told me the other night that she sits in her room reading novels all the day." And then, Caroline had added, is fulsomely charming in the evening.

"Besides," Pommy continued, "she has the headache a great deal of the time. At least she says so. I shall be surprised if she goes with us today."

The duchess turned thoughtful. She had a kind of plot working in her mind, an idea that would devastate the Mortimers and cause them to pack up at once and return to London. Since Justin was making no apparent move toward ending his engagement, then someone would have to do it for him.

Her grace was not in the least ashamed of plotting. Men were so illogical, and sometimes—as in this case—were willing to cut off their own noses to spite their faces. It would be too bad were Anilee to develop one of her headaches, but the duchess was committed to the excursion and could not cry off. At least, she could take the opportunity to use her wiles on the girl's parents, for there was no time to lose in scotching this unfortunate marriage.

But for the first time in her life, the duchess was reluctant to expose her schemes to another eye: the eye of her granddaughter. If she were forced to resort to untruths, as she had every intention of doing, she did not wish Pommy to be on hand to witness her deceit. She realized that Pommy's good opinion of her was a precious thing, and she would do nothing to tarnish it.

"My dear Pommy, I must ask you to stay here today."

Pommy, surprised, exclaimed, "Not to go with you to entertain the Mortimers? I know how greatly you dislike them. I thought I could prevent them from being a nuisance. By talking to them, I mean, and divert their attention."

"You are a precious child, my dear, and I truly am grateful for your offer. But," she continued firmly, "the barouche will be too crowded for five persons. I am persuaded you will find something to do here that will be much more amusing."

Pommy did not precisely agree with her grandmother, but with good grace she dropped the idea of accompanying her on the proposed outing. While she was at first disappointed, reflection persuaded her that several hours with Anilee would not be a happy time.

Pommy's prophecy proved true. Anilee had developed another of her headaches and begged off. Her grace responded to Lady Mortimer's apology by saying, with every indication of concern, "The poor child! I wonder whether her health is quite what it should be? So many headaches. I can recommend an excellent physician . . . in London."

The expedition covered much territory. A visit to the oldest village in Middlesex, in existence at least as far back as the ninth century, and of course the oldest church, with a pillared Norman doorway, a few old houses where the duchess claimed Dryden had visited, and Voltaire and other luminaries as well. The duchess was confirmed in her low opinion of her guests, since neither seemed to recognize the famous names she mentioned.

However, her purpose in this excursion was not to assess the intellectual level of a couple she did not intend to see again after they left Lisle Court. Instead, since she had no real leverage with Justin to bring into play, her hope was to give the Mortimers a dislike for the match. Since there could be no real reason for them to consider Justin not the son-in-law they wanted, then she must manufacture a reason.

The title, she knew, was above reproach. That left the other: money. Somehow she must contrive to cast doubt on Justin's fortune.

She began with a small remark about the Lisle Court cook. "I wonder Gaston has stayed this long, for I am sure he could find a position elsewhere."

"Why should he?" Sir Henry demanded, who had enjoyed

every bite he had put in his mouth since arriving. "I should be sorry to see him go."

"Well, no man wishes to be uncertain about his recompense."

"Uncertain? Surely he has a good salary?"

"On paper, perhaps. Look over there, if you will. That watering trough in the square is said to have been the gift of Queen Eleanor."

By gradual steps the duchess planted several hints that Justin was slow in paying his servitors, reluctant to replace the shabby furniture, and lived in rooms in London, since he did not wish the expense of renting a house.

Were they perturbed? Were they indulging in second thoughts? The duchess could not discern that her campaign of falsehood had any effect whatsoever. She dared not press too much, lest they return to Lisle Court and demand reassurances from Justin. He would not take kindly to interference, and all her efforts would make the situation worse rather than better.

It was not until Doughty drove the barouche across the bridge at the north end of the wagon road separating Edgecumbe Manor from Lisle Court that inspiration visited her.

They were traveling toward journey's end at Lisle Court, and the duchess was at her wits' end. Once renowned, at least in her own circle, for complex intrigues and fanciful deceits, she mourned inwardly at the loss of her powers. Pommy had come too late to revitalize her grandmother. Now when her talents were most needed . . .

Opportunity, in the shape of the Progg shack, knocked, and her grace was prompt to answer.

The hovel—it was little more than a hovel, since the building was due for demolition after a bright new cottage had been built for the farm worker and his family, and repairs had not been made as needed—stood at the side of the road. As the smart barouche approached, Molly and Sal came to stand next to the track.

"Oh, my," said the duchess. "I did not intend to come this way." She raised her voice to the coachman. "Doughty, do stop. I wish to speak to the little girls."

The girls looked as disreputable as the shack itself. Their dresses were sadly in need of patching, and their bare feet had not been washed since the last heavy rain. The duchess knew quite well that their parents were busy from dawn to dark in the fields until the hay was all cut and in the barn. She had also given permission, at Pommy's instigation, to allow the shack to stand until autumn saw the harvests in.

None of these considerations was transmitted to the Mortimers. Quite the opposite, in fact.

Molly cuffed her smaller sister smartly, and both dropped a curtsy. "Please, your grace," Molly said earnestly.

"You wish to speak to me?" said her grace on a note of surprise. "Of course, child. Go on."

Molly had not learned of the duchess's decision to let the shack stand for the season. She lived in fear of being transported to the village, she and Sal, where they knew no one and their parents would not return home at night because of the distance from the fields.

"Please, your grace . . ." Words failed her then and she could only gesture toward the building behind her. "Not till winter?" she managed to say.

"Of course, child," the duchess said graciously. "I cannot do anything for you now. You must ask someone else." She had so nearly mentioned Asbury's name, but fortunately she had not. The Mortimers might know the name of her farm manager. Raising her voice, she ordered Doughty to drive on to Lisle Court.

"I am sorry, Sir Henry, Lady Mortimer. I did not intend, as I said, to drive this way."

"That shack," said Sir Henry. "I wonder that you do not have it torn down."

"I quite agree it should be demolished. It will be too cold for the children in the winter. I do not like even to think about it."

"Then why—"

"Henry, it is none of our affair what her grace does with her buildings."

The duchess opened her eyes wide and looked from one to the other. "My buildings? Oh, no." She paused for effect. "I am sorry you should even think I take little care of my tenants. Truly I am most considerate of their welfare."

Sir Henry was not satisfied. "That does not bear out your statement, your grace."

"But you see, dear Sir Henry, that shack," she said earnestly, "is not on my land. It belongs, I am sorry to say, to Lord Rutledge."

There, she had lied, and lied magnificently. All, of course, in a good cause, she told her conscience.

"Since you insist, I cannot find it in my conscience to keep my knowledge to myself. This is simply another example of Justin's miserliness. It is not good management to keep one's tenants in misery. But although I have tried to suggest better ways to him, I have not succeeded."

In for a penny, in for a pound. She continued. "Of course, your daughter will have nothing to worry about. She will have her own money, doubtless, and whether Justin keeps a closed fist on his money or not, she will not suffer from it."

Eyeing her guests narrowly, the duchess believed she had at last made an impression, but of what kind she could not be sure. Certainly the Mortimers had turned thoughtful. If their marriage arrangements relied heavily on a generous allowance to be made by Justin, surely they now had much to think about.

The duchess delivered them to Lisle Court and was driven home in solitary state, well satisfied with her day.

Anilee's headache, potent enough to excuse her from her grace's excursion, vanished the moment the barouche containing her parents and the duchess was out of sight.

She had plans of her own for the afternoon, and they did not include riding over the countryside, which she loathed, in the dust and wind stirred up by an open carriage. Her time would be better spent in the company of Alexander Wolver.

Captain Wolver was well aware that his presence was not desired at Lisle Court. He was not perturbed by his cool welcome. In fact, he considered that staying in a house where no one wanted him added piquancy to his existence.

However, he knew it might be a very short time before he was asked to leave, and so far he had not got what he had come for. Anilee was about to make a splendid marriage, and would soon, he supposed, be mistress of a handsome allowance. It seemed only right that he should in some way profit from Anilee's good fortune. Had he not escorted her here and there during the past months? The laborer was worthy of his hire.

Of course, a small amount of insurance might be desirable, in the form of an indiscretion on her part that she would wish kept secret. He bent his efforts toward that accomplishment.

He had spent much time, the last few days, away from the house. He felt it unwise to call Lord Rutledge's attention to his presence. Justin's remark about not soiling his hands on the Watters fellow gave the captain reason for caution. The lord of Lisle Court was not a man to underestimate.

In his walks he had come upon a clearing suitable for his

purposes. There was a giant beech tree to provide shade, fallen logs conveniently placed to serve as benches, not too far from the house, but completely private.

There were barns and sheds, of course, nearer at hand, but from experience he considered outbuildings as traps for the unwary. Thus it was that, by arrangement, Anilee's headache had come and gone, and she and the captain were, by separate routes, converging on the clearing dominated by Pommy's mother's beech tree.

Earlier that day, when the duchess drove out toward Lisle Court, Pommy had found herself at loose ends. She was always more content out of doors, so she decided to take a book and an apple or two and spend the afternoon comfortably in her tree. None of the books she found in the manor library appealed to her this day. She sat down on the sofa in her grandmother's upstairs sitting room. Something prodded her as she sat, and she ran her hand behind the small pillows the duchess favored for her back.

She pulled out a book, thrust behind the pillows as though to conceal it. The duchess's own private reading material?

The Moorish Christian was the title. Well, thought Pommy, what is acceptable reading for the grandmother may well serve to idle away an afternoon for the granddaughter.

Consumed by curiosity, she hurried, with her apples and the book, to her refuge.

She had never seen a Minerva novel before, to say nothing of having read any. Miss Horne, that peer among governesses, had often told her, "Novel reading for young ladies is most dangerous." Dangerous? Pommy supposed she would not fall to the ground from her tree perch, and that was the only peril she could foresee from reading one book.

There was one branch of the tree that provided a secure seat for her. She could lean back comfortably against the trunk, and so luxuriant was the foliage that she was completely hidden from the ground. Soon she moved into a world she had never dreamed of. There was a castle on a mountaintop. The chambers within were rock-walled, inadequately covered by fading, shabby tapestries.

And the people! The hero—or the villain, she could not be sure—was swarthy as a Moor, but he often exclaimed, "Santa María!" The heroine had long golden hair—much like Anilee's, probably—and both she and some masked man, whoever he was, spoke in phrases that did not ring true to her.

"My angel, my heart, *mi alma, ma chère*—" He should settle down, she thought, to one language. Perhaps he could make his point better.

"Ah, my darling, we should not be here. What if he finds us?"

Pommy laid her head back against the tree and closed her eyes. What nonsense! I could write a better story myself. People don't talk like that. Nobody would say, in a breathy voice, "If he comes upon us, my darling, he will kill you."

Her eyes flew open. She had heard the words as clearly as though she were in the same gloomy castle room as the characters. And the book in her lap was closed.

Cautiously, even suspiciously, she looked around her. To her surprise, she was not alone in the clearing. Below her, clasped in an embrace that could easily have come directly from the pages of *The Moorish Christian* were Captain Wolver and Miss Anilee Mortimer.

Anilee was supposed to be driving out with the duchess, but here she was in a clandestine meeting, and not with her intended husband, either.

It was too late for her to interrupt the rendezvous. She could not appear out of the blue—or rather, the tree—without causing disorder, even chaos. In the end, she sat rigidly in the branches, praying not to succumb to an untimely sneeze, and tried to think lofty thoughts.

Her sense of right and wrong, fair and unfair, was keen. But she could not be a tittletattle. If Justin were to learn of his betrayal by Anilee, he would not learn it from Pommy.

Long after the pair had left the clearing, she sat, pondering. On her father's estate she was used to know what best to do in most circumstances. She was not accustomed to uncertainty as to the best path to pursue.

Sliding down from her tree at last, she went slowly back to the house. She had much to think about, and none of it was pleasant.

18

The day after the duchess's expedition, Lady Playre realized that time was running out.

At the time of the dinner party, a few days back, she expected the fateful announcement would be made. It seemed an appropriate time, with both families assembled and in the presence of those persons whose quality and proximity to Lisle Court might be presumed to be interested in the marriage.

Had it not been for Frederick Watters' abrupt intrusion into the entertainment—and Caroline never thought she would be grateful to him for anything—she believed she would now be assisting with wedding plans.

Since then, she had had quite enough of Anilee's tinkling voice and Lady Mortimer's crassly commercial attitude. Caroline felt as though the bailiffs had come in and were setting prices for a sale.

She had great expectations that the duchess could work a bit of magic and the arrangement would be dissolved. The Mortimers had come back from the drive yesterday, apparently unchanged, although Caroline had noticed a certain attention paid on the part of Lady Mortimer to faded spots on the carpets.

After dinner last night, Lady Mortimer noticed some loose threads from a chair seat and fingered them, a look of disapproval on her features.

Lady Playre forced a laugh. "My mother's small terrier was not well-trained, I fear. He would not let the cushions alone. But he was such comfort to my mother that no one ever scolded him."

Anilee's mother's only comment was, "Animals do not belong in the house."

Caroline held her tongue. Later, in the privacy of her own bedroom, she could not stop her tears from coming. If Anilee and her mother were to spend any time at Lisle Court, she would not come. It seemed hard to be thus exiled from her own home, the house whose every corner she knew, where she had been as happy as she had ever been. And not even to return! Such banishment was not to be borne.

While she had ached for her brother's unhappiness, now the issue cut closer to the bone. It was her own happiness she was now concerned about.

And something had to be done.

No use simply arguing with Justin on the subject. Men simply lived in a different world from women. It was astonishing, truly, that men and women ever agreed on anything long enough to marry. Probably that was why parents arranged marriages, or rather alliances as between foreign countries.

A man, she knew from her own experience, was constitutionally unable to say he had made a mistake. For example, Gervase. He was an excellent husband, as far as husbands went, but he believed devoutly that women, present company included, did not possess the ability to think.

She had mentioned to him more than once her concern about Justin's happiness. Her husband had answered comfortably, "Don't worry about him. He'll not put up with any nuisance. He'll keep her docile enough."

"Docile," she flared up. "Is docile what you look for in a wife?"

Gervase was startled. "Why would not a wife be obedient? After all, Scripture says—"

"And all you know of Scripture is what is read during the service. And you don't attend above once a month, if that. You will recall, I suppose, that the Scripture you quote was written by a man."

He realized he might have gone too far, but he had no intention of retreating. While this was not a new argument between them, under the circumstances the discussion seemed to be particularly significant.

"Docile," Caroline repeated, although on a softer note. "You do not value sweetness, loyalty, intelligence, a sweet nature—"

"You are repeating yourself," Gervase said with an air of reasonableness. "You see? Yours is not a well-trained mind."

"And whose fault is that?" she stormed, angry again. "My father—every father—refused to give his daughter the same education as a son."

"Of course not, my dear. It is not worth the trouble to educate a female. Your sex is devious, mischievous. Not to be trusted."

She stared at him, horrified. There was simply nothing she could say to penetrate his conventional view of life as it should be. Men!

But her husband was not as impervious to her opinions as he seemed. He left her, but he paused at the door and searched her features for reassurance. "Caroline? You are happy enough, aren't you?"

She greeted his overture in the only way possible—with silence.

At length he sighed and opened the door. "I think we rub along tolerably well," he said finally, and left her.

Tolerably well indeed! She as far from docile, and she had never been properly submissive to her husband. Nor would she be. Not worth educating.

She picked up whatever lay near to hand—fortunately, a pillow—and threw it hard against the door, where Gervase's head had been only moments before.

Calmer at last, she realized reluctantly that there was truth in Gervase's words. Of course women were devious. How else, given the world as it was, could they even survive? Even less could they enjoy their lives. She promised herself at that moment that if she ever had a daughter, she would fight to the death to give that child the best education possible.

Perhaps, Lady Playre thought, I could have a son first, and my daughter then could listen to his lessons, too. That was the way things had been arranged in the Harcourt family.

The dowager, Caroline decided, had been her own mistress for too long. Living in seclusion, with no one to whom she must "submit," she had lost the art of dealing with men. Caroline, on the other hand, had not.

Her mind ran on that first conversation with the duchess, when she had come up from London more than a fortnight since. All Anilee was after, they had decided together, was the title and the money. A chance phrase of her grace's recurred now to Lady Playre and lingered in her mind.

"I cannot," the duchess had said, "do anything about the title—"

Caroline sat for a long time at her dressing table, and her thoughts, as Gervase would have expected, were those of a devious and wayward mind.

* * *

Lisle Court was a large and ancient house. The larger part of the sprawling structure had been built in Stuart times, with additions tacked on haphazardly in Queen Anne's reign, and during the past century, a large wing in the graceful Georgian style was added.

The diverse character of the building resulted in certain eccentric features, many of which were not obvious to the eye, but which were well-known to the inhabitants.

For example, a private conversation carried on in the lovely cream-and-green morning room remained private so long as no one occupied the library next door or, by whimsical chance, a small storage room on the third floor. A chimney had been removed, so long ago nobody remembered when, leaving an empty shaft remarkable only for its sound-carrying qualities.

When Caroline went past the library door on her way to the morning room, she was gratified to see that Sir Henry was indeed in the library. He had formed the habit, since Justin's favorite haunt had become the study adjoining his own rooms on an upper floor, of spending his morning in the library.

She saw nobody with him and recalled that Justin had said he would be out for the day. Knowing that Anilee often spent the morning hours drinking tea in the morning room—no matter how radiant the day beyond the windows—Caroline joined her, with purpose.

With determined casualness, Lady Playre said, "Just think. Soon you will be Lady Rutledge. What a pleasant prospect!"

"Oh, my, yes."

"So many ladies in London must envy you. Although he is my brother and I am excessively fond of him, I am not blind to reality. As his wife, you will be in a position of prestige, an impeccable position.'' She eyed Anliee with speculation. ''At least, so they believe.''

''Yes, a fine position in the world.'' Her eyes shone. But her mother's tutoring held fast. ''I really care nothing for the title, you know. I have such high regard for his lordship that I must be the happiest bride in England.''

Caroline gave an ostentatious sigh of relief. She hoped Sir Henry in the library would pay attention to what she would say next. However, her audience was greater than she knew.

Justin had some days ago realized that his father's library held not one book that enticed him from the shelves or tugged at his memory. There was one book that he remembered with nostalgic pleasure, one that he had read more than once, until his father had discovered it. Justin could hear even now his father's stern voice shouting, ''*Lyrical Ballads*? Where did you get this book? My idiot bookseller sent it to me when it first came out, and I thought I had burned it. Good God, poetry! No son of mine will read such drivel.''

Justin, as usual when dealing with his father, had said nothing. Silently he said farewell to the Ancient Mariner and believed the book burned at last. But this morning, in a perverse mood, he decided to look for the book on the chance that it had once again escaped the flames. The likely place to look was a storage room on the third floor, full of trunks and old kites and a fishing rod. He changed his mind about being away all the day and ascended to the storage room to begin his search.

His happy reminiscences spent among the toys of his childhood were suddenly interrupted by hearing his name, coming so it seemed from the wall itself.

It was his sister's voice. ''I am so glad you value Justin as I do. All the rest is not important.''

Where was Caroline? She sounded as close as though she

were in the room. "The old chimney," he decided, satisfied, but who was she talking to?

Anilee agreed. "Without Lord Rutledge," she said vigorously, remembering her proper lines, "I could never be happy."

Neither Caroline nor her unseen listeners believed Anilee for a moment.

"I am so glad this grand house means little to you."

"Well, it is rather old, isn't it? I do not like old houses."

"Yes, it's been in the family for generations. Of course it won't be a wrench to you, but I grew up here." Caroline adopted a wistful expression.

Anilee's tinkling voice came again. "Of course you will always be welcome at Lisle Court. It was your father's house, after all."

"You are kind. If only Grandfather had been a man of honor."

"Honor?"

"Men set such store by honor, and then they do such shabby things."

Anilee, growing wary, spoke a little sharply. "What do you mean?"

Caroline feared her intended audience in the library might well come out and demand to know the answer to Anilee's question, in detail. She hastened on.

She needn't have worried. Anilee's father sat as though riveted to his chair. He looked across at the man in the wing chair, its back to the door, and raised his eyebrows. The other man shook his head, puzzled.

"Oh, my dear, I am sorry if I have worried you. After all, my brother did inherit a competence from our mother's family."

Anilee was shrewd enough when it came to a subject that

touched her nearly. "You're saying there's no money, except this competence?"

Caroline had not expected to do more than hint that the title was flawed. She had not intended to cast doubt on her grandfather's character, even though the dowager had said he was not a nice man. Now, in the face of Anilee's persistence, she was improvising madly and possibly without logic.

Justin thought with considerable surprise, No money? Even the mythical competence from his mother's family he knew nothing about. Entranced, he sat down on a dust-covered trunk, the better to hear. What on earth was his sister up to?

Amazingly, he was not indignant. He knew he should not sit by while Anilee was distressed, but he was intensely interested in the conversation he was overhearing.

Anilee protested. "You m-mean, he will have to sell everything?"

"Oh, no, no. Of course everything would stay in the family. It is only that another branch of the family would have it all."

"And Justin left—"

"With a competence, remember."

"I never heard of another branch of the family," Anilee said sullenly.

"I do not know quite how it is, but I believe my grandfather went through a marriage ceremony and had an heir—one he never recognized—and of course we knew nothing about him."

Caroline was grateful that Gervase did not know what she was about. She had broken rules without number in this conversation: interfering where Gervase had forbidden her to tread; maligning her grandfather, who had enjoyed the fleshpots of his time but had never contracted a secret marriage. He thought far too much of his family obligations to play such a trick on them.

Lies and deceit and mischief—all precisely as Gervase had told her. Caroline's conscience began to twist uncomfortably.

"Perhaps your father is aware of the flaw in the title. It is possible, I suppose, that seeing you had your heart set on my brother, he did not wish to deny your wish. I have noticed that your father is excessively fond of you."

At last, Anilee was showing signs of distress. "He should not have deceived me so," she said. She was recovering from Lady Playre's shocking news, and a strong instinct for survival came to her rescue.

Caroline, seeming anxious, asked, "I do hope this hasn't turned you against my brother?"

In the storage room upstairs, Justin murmured, "I hope it has."

Anilee told her, shyly but falsely, "To be honest, I am terrified of your brother. I should not dare to refuse him. My mother says he positively dotes on me. If I should refuse to marry him now, I fear he may harm himself. I should not like such a tragedy on my conscience."

Upstairs, Justin groaned. So close to being free!

Caroline saw her scheme had misfired. She was convinced that Anilee cared no more than a snap of her fingers for Justin. Justin do harm for himself? What nonsense!

She tried once more. "But he is—" The words stuck in her throat, but after all, Anilee's father in the library next door was the only one who could hear. "I would think you would recoil from marrying a fraud."

Anilee had regained her poise. She rose and said prettily, in her insipid tinkling voice, "Ah, but this other has not been proven, has it? And until it is, I shall be Lady Rutledge, with my gowns and my furs and my London house."

With a last sweet smile, she floated from the room, leaving

Caroline speechless with fury. After a few moments, she calmed herself. If her dear papa heard all he was supposed to hear, he might himself call off the wedding.

She rang for tea to be brought to the morning room. She intended to give Sir Henry every chance to emerge from the library, doubtless choleric of face and high of temper, and seek out his daughter or, more likely, his host. Fortunately, Justin had remarked at breakfast he was riding to the other end of his estates for the day.

She was pleased to hear the library door open, followed by rapid footsteps fading away in the opposite direction. Sir Henry was rising to the bait. Maybe all was not yet lost.

The door behind her opened abruptly. The maid with the tea she had asked for, no doubt. She must be one of the newer servants, for she had not yet learned to open a door soundlessly.

She looked up. Gervase, as red of face as ever Sir Henry could have been, stood in the doorway.

"Good God, Madam," he shouted at her, "what are you about?"

"Gervase?" she said weakly. "Where have you come from?"

"From the library. Do you know that every word spoken in this room is clear as day in the next room?"

"What did you hear?" she whispered, appalled.

"Every word. The walls are thin as paper. I can tell you Mortimer was as stunned as I was." He slammed the door behind him, not noticing a maid on his heels bringing the tea Caroline expected, and advanced a few feet into the room. Standing over his wife and fixing her with a baleful and bulging eye, he said ominously, "Well, madam?"

Her only defense was to stand her ground. "I should think you would be ashamed to confess you listened to a private conversation, Gervase. It is not like you."

"Is there a problem with the inheritance?"

Her knees were shaking abominably, but she managed to retort, "You and Papa made all the arrangements for our marriage. Didn't you make sure, with your logical minds, that all was in order then?"

Her husband pulled himself, with visible effort, together. He took a deep breath and spoke, this time with a deliberate and measured calmness she found quite terrifying.

"If there is not a flaw in the title, you have lied to Miss Mortimer, and I shall expect you to apologize. If there is, then you have deceived me and I shall need to consult the proper attorneys."

He turned on his heel and left the room, slamming the door behind him, leaving his wife to bury her face in her hands and give herself over to uncontrollable sobbing.

Poor Caroline, thought Justin upstairs in the storage room, and returned to his study, his cherished *Lyrical Ballads* in his hand and his mind at last at peace.

19

Pommy was troubled in her mind.

Burdened as she was with the knowledge of Anilee
Mortimer's clandestine meeting under the beech tree while
Pommy was a captive audience a dozen feet above the
ground, she did not know what to do. If Anilee were willing
to betray Justin even before they were formally betrothed,
there seemed little chance for him to enjoy a happy marriage.

Pommy knew that she herself had far too great an interest
in Justin's welfare for her to be impartial. Had she jumped
to erroneous conclusions as to the significance of Anilee's
behavior?

Carefully she reviewed, over the next few days, exactly
what she knew.

Her grandmother had told her that Anilee suffered from
the headache and could not accompany her parents on the
duchess's excursion. Pommy had seen no sign of headache
in the young lady who sped into the clearing straight into
the arms of the captain.

Into his arms? Pommy flushed with embarrassment. The
scene enacted only a few feet from her had indicated without
possibility of doubt that Anilee and Captain Wolver were

not meeting, alone, for the first time. And Pommy helplessly kept her knowledge to herself.

For one thing, she did not wish to confess that she was guilty of eavesdropping, even though she could not have prevented it. She could hardly have dropped from the sky into the middle of a lovers' rendezvous, could she?

For another, she was no tittletattle. Gentlemen may have their honor, about which they are often tediously prosy, but ladies too knew right from wrong. Wryly, she thought, ladies did not always follow the righteous paths that were dictated, but at least they knew what they were.

There must be a way to convey information to Justin, a way that would enlighten him but also would leave any decision to him to make. He must see with his own eyes, she thought. Hearsay was not always convincing.

Also, Pommy had no wish to appear as a principal in this disclosure. She had more than a casual interest in Justin's happiness. If he did not reciprocate her feelings, she knew she would mourn for her loss all her life.

Since her education was almost entirely classical, she searched her memory for a device that would serve. The gods and goddesses availed themselves often of their powers of disguise. Athena, for example, turned herself into an old crone to chastise the boastful weaver Arachne. But that device was beyond Pommy's powers.

Besides, she thought, the deities on Mount Olympus would in all likelihood range themselves at Anilee's side. Remembering the frank earthiness of Zeus, for example, Pommy gave up on the classics. What good was an education if it did not serve when one was desperate for answers?

To divert her thoughts, she again picked up *The Moorish Christian*. Much as she wanted to read the entire novel in one sitting, she dared not. Despite the poor writing she had gotten well-snared by the first chapters before she had been interrupted by the rendezvous below her. Now, reading hastily to finish the book before the duchess missed it, she raced excitedly through deserted apartments lit by decaying lamps, false assignations, mysterious meetings, and arrived at the last page drained of emotion, but with the brightest of plans germinating in her mind.

Novels, her governess had informed her loftily, were trash, fit only for an untrained mind. Pommy found herself using a term of her grandmother's: "Pooh to that!" Thanks to that "trash," she knew just how to unravel her dilemma.

Early the next morning, she addressed herself to composing the appropriate notes. Her plan was to reenact the tryst, setting a time of four o'clock that afternoon, and make sure that Justin came upon the pair. If, then, he chose to keep to his agreement, there was no hope for him. Or for her.

Finally, the notes were completed. One was to go to Anilee, purporting to be from Captain Wolver. The second was from Wolver to Anilee.

The third note, to Justin, required the most concentration. Half a dozen sheets of paper lay crumpled in the waste basket before she was satisfied. How to sign it? Finally she settled on "A Friend," under the mistaken impression that the *nom de plume* was a sufficient disguise for her identity.

With a great sigh of relief and a good deal of apprehension, she dispatched the notes to Lisle Court and composed herself to abide in suspense until the appointed hour.

The day that Pommy set her plan in motion was the same day that Lady Playre launched her own scheme to persuade Anilee that a life with Justin was not her best choice.

When Justin descended from the storage room to his study, his mind was made up. He was grateful to his sister for her timely plotting, but he himself preferred to meet obstacles face to face. He sent for Captain Wolver.

Within thirty minutes, the captain left Lisle Court. He understood Justin's strong suggestion that he not trouble any of the other guests by saying farewell to them.

Sir Henry Mortimer, on the other hand, needed no persuasion, having made up his mind an hour since. He had been increasingly uneasy about trusting his only daughter to Lord Rutledge. Her grace the duchess had not wanted to tell him the whole of it, but he was no fool—he could read between the lines. The duchess had told him far more than she was aware of, he believed. The cap of it all was that conversation overheard from the library. A good thing, he thought righteously, that he could see which way the wind blew. Even more fortunate was the fact that he had discovered the shaky foundations of the Harcourt family before he had signed anything.

He sought out his host in the upstairs study.

"Lord Rutledge, thank God you are not out on your estates as I was led to believe this morning. Although after what I saw the other day, I am not surprised that you laze the day away indoors."

Justin, rightly, was astonished. "I do not . . . laze, did you say?"

"I have her grace to thank for having my eyes opened. What I saw of your estates gives me pause. I would not have wished you to be a spendthrift, of course, but decent landowners keep their tenants—" He stopped short. Justin's expression was completely blank.

"You don't know what I am speaking about, do you?" Sir Henry continued in an altered voice. "The more shame to you, then. You must not blame her grace for confiding too much in me. She did not wish to do so."

Justin, who had risen when his guest entered, sank slowly

into the leather chair behind the desk. He had sustained sufficient shock that morning when he overheard his sister's outrageous scheme. Now he learned it was possible that the duchess had entered the lists along with Caroline with some kind of wild tale. Were they all planning his life for him? It came to him, with unexpected warmth, that he must be held in some affection, or these ladies would not trouble themselves on his behalf.

"Perhaps," he said faintly, "you had best tell me what she said."

"Willingly," Sir Henry said. "We went out for that drive the other day, you know. On the way home we came up some road, a wide wagon road. I daresay you know which one I mean." Justin nodded. "Well, then, you will also recognize the shack I speak of."

He described what could only be, Justin realized, the Progg shack. "What about that cottage?"

"Cottage, you say. Hovel, I call it. I confess I have a much smaller estate than you have here, but my buildings are kept up and my tenants are warm in the winter. Not like the inhabitants of that shack. Two little girls stood in the road beside that building, begging us to help them before the cold weather."

"But what does that shack have to do . . ." Justin stopped short. Nearly too late, he recognized the duchess's fine intriguing hand. He knew well her plans for the Progg cottage. None of her grace's tenants went hungry or cold. But to foist the apparent ownership on him—it was really too bad of her grace.

Justin could recognize an opportunity when one arose before him. He spoke truly, however, when he murmured, "I am sorry her grace chose to confide in you."

"A good thing she did. Besides, I do not hesitate to tell you that what I overheard just now from the library was enough for me, no matter how miserly you are. Do you know the walls of that room are thin as paper? Well, my lord, what answer do you have?''

"I think I know the idiosyncrasies of this house as well as anyone," Justin said quietly. "Was that your question?"

"No, it was not!" Sir Henry was choleric. "My question, sir, is how do you explain your neglect, your inhumanity about your tenants, and how do you explain that flawed title, the one you said not a word about when we spoke about my daughter's settlement?"

"Do you know," Justin said slowly, "I don't think I will."

Sir Henry eyed him narrowly. "So. Very well, then. I will ask that you consider your betrothal to my daughter at an end."

"Indeed I shall," Justin said promptly. "We may all count ourselves fortunate to discover in time that the marriage will not suit."

Sir Henry snorted. "My Anilee can do better than this, though I suppose it is unhandsome of me to say so." He moved to the door. "We shall not trespass on your hospitality beyond early afternoon." Justin bowed. "I shall take steps to ensure that you do not deceive other innocents. Some females do not have an adequate masculine protector, you know."

Sir Henry opened the door and was halfway through it when Justin's deliberately quiet voice reached him. "Sir Henry, do I understand that you do not wish me to marry your daughter?"

"Good God, could I have put it more plainly?"

"That is your irrevocable decision?"

"Yes."

"I do hope you will not see fit to tell this tale in London. I would be forced then, you know, to defend my good name."

"Good name!" But Sir Henry, sensing that he was about to hear unwelcome news, said no more.

"Both counts on which you accuse me are nonsense. A pure taradiddle."

"How can this be? Her grace said—"

"And you, Sir Henry, were taken in by the duchess and my sister without the suspicion of a doubt. You believed a pair of women before you put trust in me or my man of affairs in London. Understand me, Sir Henry. You will hold your tongue on this head, now and in the future, or be revealed as a gullible fool."

Sir Henry seemed smaller than a moment ago. "Then none of that was true?"

"Not a word. In fact," Justin said with a grin, "the shack belongs, not to me, but to her grace."

Sir Henry, a defeated man, closed the door quietly behind him.

Justin rejoiced. For the first time in months, no weighty burden sat on his shoulders.

Lunch was a quiet meal at Lisle Court. Only the Mortimers sat at the table in the dining room. Captain Wolver had already departed and the Mortimer luggage was stacked in the hall.

Lady Playre, unable to remain longer in the morning room, where she was acutely conscious of her failure not only to liberate Justin but also to maintain her marriage, moved to the back sitting room, where she drank several cups of tea without being comforted.

She had never seen Gervase so enraged. Coupled with his righteous anger, spilled hotly over her head, her own conscience took sides against her. Of course she was guilty of lying, of interfering, of whatever else Gervase wished to accuse her. But she had thought the cause was a worthy one.

Never before had he mentioned lawyers. A divorce petition would, by virtue of their rank, be received and judgment rendered by the House of Lords. The alternative, and that not one she could count on, was to apologize to Anilee. Degrading as that might be, it had to be done. Even if she groveled at Anilee's smartly shod feet, she had no guarantee that Gervase would relent.

After seeing the Mortimers fed, bundled into their carriage, and sent on their way, Justin looked for his sister. He had, in a surprising turn of temperament, cleared his house of nuisances. He had not known it would be so easily done, nor that he would feel so liberated, such a master of his own life.

His father's arrangements for his marriage were nullified. One by one, he believed, other lingering encumbrances from the past might well fall like dominoes. But his most important need, at the moment, was to settle his fate with Pommy.

First, however, he found Caroline in the back sitting room. This was a cheerful room where his mother had spent much of her time. It had not been altered since her death.

Caroline was sitting in a chair next to the broad window, some papers in her hand, and looking out into the garden. She did not look up when he came in, and he did not think she knew he was there.

"Caroline?"

After a moment she turned to look at him. "What is it, Justin? I am not quite in the mood for conversation."

He sat in a chair opposite. "I know."

"What do you know?" She roused herself. "Did you come back early?"

"I didn't ride out at all. I was in the storage room on the third floor."

The sparkle had gone from her eyes, he saw with a pang.

He was extremely fond of his sister and disliked seeing her unhappy. Now, of course, she was far more than unhappy. She was desolate.

"Caroline, I heard everything. How foolish of you to mount such a prank."

"Justin, I do not need your scolding."

"I am not scolding, my dear. I am so grateful that you care enough about me to—"

"To hazard everything, even my marriage? Dear brother, you flatter yourself. I did not know the risk."

"Gervase will come around."

"I wonder. It's all a matter of honor, you see. First there was your foolish clinging to a plan that you did not even make yourself. Your honor was at stake, you said. And you plunged headlong into disaster."

"Caroline—"

"And Gervase, he knows there's nothing wrong with the title. But he feels that because I lied—all in a good cause, you know—somehow my behavior reflects on him. And his precious honor."

"You're his wife, and whatever you do he is responsible for."

"A mere scheme, played out in the family? I can see that he might be justified if I were to take up with Queen Caroline against her husband. But for this?" She was silent for a little while. Then she resumed, on a different note. "Do you know, I have come to think very little of honor. Both you, Justin, and Gervase may find your honor very cold comfort in the years ahead. And I for one will not feel in the least sorry for you."

She rose. She looked at the papers in her hand as though she did not know what they were.

Justin rose too. "Dear Caroline—" He made to embrace her, but she moved aside. "I came in to thank you for what you did. I have thrown Wolver out and the Mortimers have just left.''

"Left? Then the betrothal is canceled?''

"I finally got the courage to call it off.''

She frowned at the papers in her hand and gave them to her brother. "I remember now. Hibbert gave me these letters. They came by hand, he said. But since they are addressed to persons who are no longer under your roof, Justin, I pray you do with them what you will.''

She opened the door and stepped into the hall. She had immense dignity, Justin realized, and wrapped in his own affairs, he had never noticed before.

She paused and said with the slow deliberation of an old woman, "I wish you had made up your mind on this head a little sooner.''

He watched her down the hall, walking without her usual springy step. Just so had his mother walked in her old age, heavily, and with resignation to her fate.

20

He had much to answer for, he knew.

Now that he had gotten past the brightly shining shield of honor, seeing the falseness of his conception of an admirable virtue, Justin felt as though he saw all things clearly for the first time.

He was tempted to put the blame for the arrangement with Anilee entirely upon his father's shoulders, but he knew he was as guilty as anyone. He could have refused at the start.

But of course he couldn't have.

Still, it did no good to dwell on the unfortunate past. He had felt sorry for himself, and in his morose brooding he had inspired those who loved him to unwarranted scheming on his behalf—all because of what he had called his "honor."

And see what that had led to. He suspected the duchess was bearing up well under whatever lies she had told. A geographical genius—putting the dilapidated Progg cabin, due to be torn down at the end of harvest time, squarely on his land and to his discredit.

But closer to his heart was the disaster that had befallen Caroline. Even though she had in a sense brought it on herself, still he bore a heavy weight of guilt.

An honorable man must make amends for his sins.

He stood where his sister had left him, in the back sitting room with three letters in his hands. Automatically he glanced at them. One was addressed to Anilee, a second to Captain Wolver. His own name leapt out at him from the third. Delivered by hand? There was a puzzle here, but it must wait. He set out in search of his brother-in-law.

He ran Gervase to ground in the library, that ill-fated room whose walls were no thicker than a heavy curtain. If his plans went as he hoped, he would spend most of his days here at Lisle Court, enjoying the country life that suited him. He could add thick paneling to the walls in the interests of privacy. But he and P—that is, he would have no need for privacy. Superstitiously, he refused to mention the name of the lady he planned to offer for as soon as he could ride over to Edgecumbe Manor. It was entirely possible, considering some of the accusations she had hurled at him during their short acquaintance, that she would reject him.

He needed to set his own house in rights first.

"There you are," he said heartily, crossing the room to sit down opposite Gervase.

"Where else?" Gervase said with a hint of a snarl. "My marriage in shambles, your sister behaving in a most outrageous manner. I vow your mother would not countenance such wanton conduct."

"Wanton?" Justin bristled. "Outrageous, I grant you. Irresponsible, no doubt of it. But wanton? I think not."

"What maggot got into her head? I vow I cannot understand a woman like Caroline."

Justin considered. Judiciously, he finally answered. "You know, I think we make a mistake in trying to understand women."

Gervase looked up quickly. "Then you don't comprehend them either?"

"I don't try. Caroline was wrong in what she did, of

course. She should not have lied. But I wish my conscience were clear on that head, for I have not always told nothing but the truth.''

''But this was so unnecessary.''

Justin was enjoying the cleansing relief of a new convert who had put his past mistakes behind him. He wished the world to share his intoxicated state of mind.

''Of course it was unnecessary, but whose fault was that? Mine! If I had not been stupid and obstinate, she would not have even been tempted to such a drastic measure. Our grandfather indeed had a certain cavalier attitude toward propriety, but he never betrayed the inheritance.'' He studied Gervase. He could not detect any lightening of the man's misery. ''Was that your concern? That Caroline's dowry might be diminished?''

At last a spark of anger emerged. ''Good God, Justin, no! But I told her not to interfere—''

''I'm very pleased that she did. I overheard the entire conversation, you know.''

''But you weren't in the library.''

''I was someplace else.'' Even now, he did not enjoy baring his shabby eavesdropping behavior. ''Any reasonable man—that is you, Gervase—would not have been taken in by that taradiddle for a minute. Fortunately, Sir Henry is a fool.''

''He believed her?''

''Indeed he did. So, you see, I owe my present freedom to my sister. She was right all the time.''

A long silence fell between them. Gervase finally spoke. ''Then you think I should forgive Caroline?''

''What is there to forgive? She acted unselfishly, for my best interests, and she was right. She deserves better than a husband who sees only that she disobeyed his ill-advised orders.''

Justin had said all he knew to say. If Gervase did not make up his quarrel with his sister, Justin himself would forever carry a burden of guilt. He rose to leave. At the door he paused. "If you think her scheme an outrageous one, I will tell you some time what the duchess did."

Somewhat to his surprise, Justin found the three letters still in his hand. An honorable man would not have read them. If Anilee and the captain were within reach, he certainly would have delivered them, unopened.

However, under the circumstances . . .

The contents of the notes that Pommy had carefully crafted gave rise to speculation of a high order. He had no doubt, considering the planned rendezvous was to take place in the beech-tree clearing, that Pommy had taken a hand in the several intrigues designed for his liberation. Anilee and the captain to meet at the beech tree, the note addressed to himself from "A Friend" designed to place him also in the clearing only half an hour from now, as a spectator? Pommy had a long way to go before she was as skilled in machinations as her grandmother.

He sighed. It would be up to him, if she would marry him, to surround her with such care and indulgence that she would never need to refine her plotting instincts. If he had needed a sign to tell him that Pommy cared a fig for him, that sign was contained in the notes. He set out for the clearing with a light heart.

Gervase had much to think about. Listening to Justin's explanations, he became aware that his anger had, unnoticed, slipped away, and all that was left to him was his deep affection for his wife. He was surprised at its strength. For the first time he realized that the tables were turned. From his initial hot indignation, even threatening divorce, he had come a complete circle. Now his fear was that his wife might spurn him for his lack of sympathy, his lack of trust in her.

Now, an anxious man, he climbed the stairs to the sitting room of their suite. He tapped on the closed door of their bedroom. Hearing no response, he gently eased the door open.

The room was dark, but he could discern the figure of his wife on the big bed across the room.

"Caroline?" He spoke softly, in a voice she had not heard since their wedding night. She stirred and he entered the room, closing the door firmly behind him.

Pommy came early to the tree.

On this occasion she carried no book, expecting the activity to take place in the clearing—if her notes bore the anticipated fruit—to be as engrossing and in all likelihood as tragic as any novel. She ached for the pain Justin would feel, betrayed by the woman he should most trust.

She wished she had rejected her plot out of hand.

Finally comfortable on her favorite branch, her back against the solid trunk, she took an apple from her pocket and began to eat. It was just as well that she was prepared for a long wait, since nobody came.

She judged that the time she had mentioned in her notes had come and gone. What had gone wrong? Anilee had certainly been eager to see Captain Wolver on the previous occasion. Suppose Anilee had met the captain privately and they discovered that someone else had written the notes. Certainly they would avoid the clearing at all costs.

And what of Justin? He too must be too wary to fall into her trap. As a plotter, she was a failure. She suspected that the plot of *The Moorish Christian* contained flaws not noticeable to the naïve eye of the reader.

She did not know how long she had perched on her branch.

Now she wished she had brought a book with her. She decided she would wait a bit longer before giving up and returning to the house.

The afternoon air was quiet. Leaves stirred to a fitful breeze, and in the home woods even the birdsong was muted. Far away she could hear approaching trotting hoofbeats and wheels on the road. Surely the two persons she expected first would not come by the road?

But the horses were slowing. Whoever traveled along the road was stopping. She leaned forward and separated the branches to see better. Unnoticed, her apple core fell to the ground.

Two men descended from a curricle. There was something oddly familiar about them. One of them, the taller, opened the gates and, walking along the wagon road with purpose, approached the beech tree. They stopped—to her dismay—directly below her.

In fact, the taller of the men, who seemed to be in charge, leaned against the trunk. If he had reached up, he might have reached the toe of her slipper. She forced herself not to move, lest her presence be discovered.

"I wondered whether the old tree still stood," the man said.

If she thought him familiar from the distance, it was to be expected. Sir Arthur Fiske, who was, as far as she knew, digging up a temple in the Aegean, stood near enough to touch.

She had a feeling that the world had tilted, and then she recovered. Her father! Here in the clearing that she thought was private to her mother and herself, and, of course, assorted lovers. And, speaking of lovers, her father's companion was Frederick Watters.

Her breath stopped. Her father had come all the way back to England to force her to marry Frederick. Oh, she was undone! Her grandmother would not allow it, but her father had the sole right to marry her where he would.

"The old lady," her father was saying when she attended to him again, "brought Julia here from Woodburn, thinking she was keeping her safe from me. But Julia and I used to meet here, made our plans to elope here, and her grace—the old tyrant!—never knew a thing until we were gone."

A new light on her mother, thought Pommy—clandestine lovers, flouting convention in pursuit of their happiness. And Pommy might be forced to follow her mother's example, except that Pommy would be running away from marriage, not toward it.

She had been so engrossed in the unexpected activity below her that she had not heard Justin approaching until she caught sight of him at the edge of the clearing.

"Good God, it's Rutledge," cried Frederick. "I mean you no harm, your lordship. I simply accompanied Sir Arthur—"

Justin ignored him. "You are Sir Arthur Fiske?" He advanced toward him, hand outstretched. "I am Rutledge."

"I came," insisted Frederick, "only because it is my curricle and my cattle."

Sir Arthur took the hand offered him. "I remember your father, but not well. Our paths did not often cross."

"I imagine not, Sir Arthur. My father did not move much in society."

Pommy's father was searching his memory. "Your mother was a lovely lady."

"Yes, she was, wasn't she?" Justin seemed to notice Frederick for the first time. "I trust you have no intention of harassing Miss Fiske again?"

Sir Arthur gave a hoot of laughter. "I think my daughter will have something to say about that. I understand she was the source of some damage to him? I wish I had seen it."

Justin was finding Pommy's father quite different from

what he expected. As long as the man seemed not to take him in aversion, he might well move quickly ahead in the way he wanted to go. "I don't understand you, sir," Justin said. "I understood that you approved of Pommy's marriage to this—that is, to Watters here?"

"All a bunch of nonsense. I wouldn't consider it for a moment."

"Lady Derwent assured my sister that you had written her—"

Sir Arthur turned on his young cousin. "Is that true? She said that?" Frederick's expression was sufficient answer. "Lies, Rutledge. Can't believe a word that woman says, even if she is my cousin. My daughter is not betrothed to anyone. I have too much regard for her to countenance a bad marriage."

"Pommy does not think you know she's alive."

"Well, she's wrong. I do." Suddenly a thought struck him. He surveyed Justin from toe to crown. "You, Rutledge. Are you married?"

Amused, Justin assured him he was not. The man was crude in his direct approach, and Lord Rutledge feared what he might say next. Nonetheless, such straightforward honesty was, in light of recent events, a refreshing change.

"But I hope you will look with favor upon my suit."

"You want to marry my daughter?"

Justin said in a slightly louder voice, "More than anything in the world."

Sir Arthur appeared to consider for a moment. Then he thrust out his hand to Justin. "I've no objection to that." He nodded curtly to Frederick. "Come along. We're on our way to Edgecumbe Manor." He gave his prospective son-in-law a wicked wink. "I've got a surprise for her grace. Even she can't object to you."

He had a parting word for Lord Rutledge. "Maybe you

can get the emeralds away from her. They belong to Pommy now, you know."

Justin leaned against the huge beech trunk. The sounds of the departing rig died away in the distance, and silence settled over the clearing.

At length, he said softly, "Pommy, you can come down now."

There was a quick indrawn breath above his head. He turned and she slid down into his arms.

"How did you know I was here?"

"The apple core there on the ground. A fresh one."

"Why did you come?"

"I received your note. As well as your notes to Miss Mortimer and Captain Wolver."

She gasped. "You—you got them all?"

"Of course. Since my agreement with regard to Anilee had been broken, the Mortimers left Lisle Court directly after lunch today. And Wolver is of no account. What was I to do with your notes? I am persuaded that Anilee would not wish a letter of such compromising content sent to her in London."

"It was a foolish thing to do," Pommy said morosely. She made as though to move away, but he held her tight.

"Does this remind you of something?"

She nodded. "You should have let me go, then. My problems were not yours."

"They are now," he told her, gravely. "My darling . . ." After a well-spent interval, he asked shakily, "And you will not run away again?"

"From you? Not ever."

"Perhaps I should take you back to the manor now."

She tightened her clasp around his neck. Her grandmother had been her salvation, and she loved her dearly. But her father was doubtless engaging the duchess that very moment in a verbal fencing match, to their mutual satisfaction, and she was sure she would not be missed.

Her grandmother had also enlarged her vocabulary. Pommy tightened her clasp around Justin's neck and reached up to kiss him.

"Pooh to that," she said.